'I'll let you know what I want in return for—helping you out in this way.'

Kenzie felt the colour drain from her cheeks. 'What you want in return...?' she repeated carefully.

'Of course,' Dominick ⸺ didn't seriously think I ⸺ ⸺ience myself in this ⸺

She hadn't ⸺ all, beyond getting him t⸺ to the wedding on Saturday!

He shook his head as he stared at her. 'How naïve you still are, Kenzie,' he taunted. 'I'll give it some thought in the next few days and let you know what I decide is an appropriate payment.'

Carole Mortimer was born in England, the youngest of three children. She began writing in 1978, and has now written over ninety books for Harlequin Mills and Boon. Carole has four sons, Matthew, Joshua, Timothy and Peter, and a bearded collie called Merlyn. She says, 'I'm happily married to Peter senior; we're best friends as well as lovers, which is probably the best recipe for a successful relationship. We live in a lovely part of England.'

THE BILLIONAIRE'S MARRIAGE BARGAIN

BY
CAROLE MORTIMER

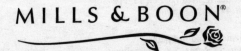

First published in Great Britain 2007
Harlequin Mills & Boon Limited,
Eton House, 18-24 Paradise Road, Richmond, Surrey TW9 1SR

© Carole Mortimer 2007

ISBN-13: 978 0 263 85346 9

Set in Times Roman 10½ on 12½ pt
01-0807-44541

Printed and bound in Spain
by Litografia Rosés, S.A., Barcelona

THE
BILLIONAIRE'S
MARRIAGE
BARGAIN

CHAPTER ONE

DOMINICK scowled HIS displeasure as the intercom on his desk buzzed, totally interrupting his train of thought. He should have told his secretary he didn't want to be disturbed for a couple of hours. After four months of careful planning, he was now on the brink of achieving his goal, and had been sitting behind his desk in his penthouse office overlooking the Thames, relishing that thought in peace and solitude.

Four months. It had seemed longer. Much longer. But to have rushed in four months ago, without giving the problem his usual careful attention, wouldn't have made the revenge he was now planning half as sweet.

Revenge, he had once been told, was a dish best eaten cold. He was cold now, icily so, and intended savouring every minute of the downfall of the man who had wounded his pride four months ago, when he had taken Kenzie from him.

Dominick turned his chair from the magnificent view outside to press the intercom, the irritation audible in his transatlantic drawl. 'Yes?'

'Mrs Masters on line one, Dominick,' Stella, his

stalwart secretary informed him, totally unconcerned by his obvious impatience with her interruption.

His mother was phoning him?

Although why the hell she still called herself Masters, when she had been married—and divorced—twice more after divorcing his father thirty years ago, Dominick had no idea!

'Tell her I'm busy,' he rasped.

'I did,' Stella came back unruffled. 'But she says it's urgent.'

He sighed his annoyance. 'Remind me to forget your Christmas bonus this year,' he muttered, cutting off Stella's knowing chuckle as he accepted the call. 'Mum,' he greeted tersely. 'Whatever it is, can you make it quick? I have—'

'Dominick.'

Everything stopped. Movement. Breathing.

Just his name, uttered in that sexily husky tone, was still enough to bring his well-ordered world briefly to a halt.

He hadn't seen or spoken to Kenzie in four months, and he had no idea why she should be telephoning him now. Although the coincidence of it, when he was so close to exacting his revenge, didn't escape him…

'Dominick?'

Not his mother, after all.

But the woman whom until recently, he had called his wife. Who was still his wife. Even if she had left him to be with another man. The man Dominick was so re-lishing bringing to his knees.

He drew in a sharp breath, and his dark gaze nar-rowed. 'Kenzie,' he acknowledged abruptly.

Kenzie easily recognized that coldly forbidding tone.

The ice man was what she had called him during the argument that had preceded the end of their brief marriage.

Argument?

No, there hadn't been an argument, she acknowledged heavily, only Dominick's coldness and her own disbelief at his accusations.

Her hand tightened defensively about her mobile. She hadn't wanted to make this call. She would rather have done anything than make the first move after these months of silence, aware that Dominick had hated her when she'd left, and knowing him well enough to realize that his hatred would only have increased during that time.

'Well?' he snapped his impatience with her silence.

It was the same old Dominick, she thought. He was always impatient, always caught up in some business deal or other, never having the time to listen, to even try to understand her.

Her shoulders tensed before she quickly shook off these negative thoughts. There was no point in going there. Nothing had changed. She hadn't. And Dominick certainly hadn't.

She hadn't been absolutely sure when she'd made the call that he was in London at the moment, but she could picture him now, sitting behind the glass-topped desk in his luxurious ultra-modern office. The building he worked in was sumptuous recognition of the highly diversified multimillion-pound Masters empire Dominick had made. As well as owning his own airline, a television company and a casino in the South of France, he also had exclusive hotels in all the major capitals of the world.

Yes, she could picture her husband now, with his dark, slightly overlong hair, brooding brown eyes that could turn black during strong emotion, arrogant slash of a nose, and fine chiselled lips above a squarely determined jaw. His wide shoulders, tapered waist and long, long legs would be dressed in one of the expensively tailored suits he bought from Italy, while his shoes would be handmade from the same country.

Just thinking of the way Dominick looked was still enough to make her heart beat erratically and the palms of her hands become damp—

'Either tell me why you called, Kenzie, or get off the damned line; I have work to do,' Dominick barked uncompromisingly.

'So what's new?' she retorted.

'Well?' His impatience was barely suppressed now as he refused to respond to her sarcasm.

But hearing Kenzie's voice again like this, completely out of the blue, was not conducive to pleasant conversation.

Not that there had been any chance of that anyway where Kenzie was concerned. None of his emotions had ever been lukewarm where Kenzie was involved. Fierce desire the first time he looked at her. Cold fury when she walked out of his life into the arms of another man.

'I—need to talk to you, Dominick,' she told him quietly.

His mouth twisted. 'Isn't it a little late for talking? I received the divorce papers a month ago,' he added harshly.

He had received them, and put them away in his desk drawer unanswered.

But maybe that was what she wanted to talk to him about…

Was she really in so much of a hurry, so desperate to

legally end their marriage, that she was even willing to speak to him personally in order to get a positive response?

Because she already had husband number two lined up…?

Jerome Carlton, of course, the man she had left him to be with, who was no doubt willing to give her everything Dominick couldn't. Was Kenzie actually thinking of marrying another man before the ink was dry on their own divorce papers?

He should never have actually married her, having never thought marriage was in his plans for the future at all until he met her.

After witnessing the mess his parents had made of their own marriage, plus their subsequent ones, Dominick had never considered getting married himself, and had certainly never wanted to bring a child into that minefield of emotions. His own childhood had been a nightmare of pseudo stepfathers and stepmothers, none of which had lasted very long.

But around fourteen months ago he had met Kenzie at a party in London to celebrate the opening of yet another Masters hotel, and it had taken just one look at the tall, beautiful, internationally famous model for him to decide he was going to have her in his bed. Her beauty was dazzling, her sensuality enough to send his pulse racing and, as a woman reputed to remain aloof from any sort of affair, she had been a challenge.

Dominick had wined and dined her, becoming more and more intrigued by her every time he had seen her. As he had got to know her better—and desire her to the point of madness—he had also come to realize the reason for her lack of physical involvements. Despite

Kenzie's glamorous, high-profile lifestyle as one of the highest paid models in the world, underneath it all she was still just the girl from the small village in England where her parents still lived and Kenzie and her three sisters had been born and grown up. The sophistication was just a façade, and what she believed in, and was waiting for was that elusive happy-ever-after.

It was a fact that had been completely borne out when he had tried to make love to her and discovered that she had still been a virgin, and saving herself for Mr Right. She had had no intention of becoming involved in a short-term affair, with him or any other man.

Quite what madness had possessed Dominick when she'd told him this, he still wasn't sure. Perhaps it had been a need to possess, to have someone who was unique in his previous world of transient relationships that meant nothing to him or the women involved, a need to know that no other man had had, or ever would have, Kenzie. All he knew for certain was that the burning need for Kenzie to be his had intensified to the point that even his business had suffered from his lack of attention as he had seemed to think of taking her to bed day and night— something he had never allowed to happen before!

It had been a situation he had known couldn't continue.

Which had left him with one solution.

Marriage…

Why not? he had reasoned once he'd got over the initial shock that he had even been considering such a move. He would never be stupid enough to fall in love, and so leave himself open to the pain and disillusion-ment his parents had inflicted on each other over the years of their marriage and since.

He was thirty-seven years old, he had reasoned at the time, and taking a wife, especially a beautiful and accomplished one like the international model Kenzie Miller, as well as putting her in his bed, could also be an astute business move. The fact that he wasn't in love with Kenzie, and that he was determined never to love any woman, had never come into his calculations.

It was something he had come to regret only nine months after they were married when Kenzie had left him for a man who obviously could give her what she wanted!

For her part, Kenzie was glad this conversation was taking place over the telephone, relieved Dominick couldn't see the pallor of her face, and the strain about her eyes and mouth created just from talking to him again.

She had taken one look at Dominick and fallen in love with him, and had been completely knocked off her feet when he had returned that interest. The two of them had been inseparable for the next few weeks, before Dominick had totally surprised her by whisking her off to Las Vegas in his private jet and marrying her.

She had felt a momentary flash of regret at the time that her parents and sisters couldn't be at the wedding, knowing that her family would be disappointed too. She was sure her parents had always thought she would have a similar traditional white wedding, to those her two younger sisters had had when they married.

But she had been so much in love with Dominick, and had secretly longed to be his wife, that she had quickly forgotten those regrets in the wonder of having her dream come true as they had spent two weeks completely alone on the Caribbean island that he owned.

What she had failed to realize for some months after they were married was that although Dominick had asked her to marry him he didn't actually return her love. He had only fallen in lust with her, and considered her a business asset as much as anything else.

And none of these painful memories was helping her situation now!

'I didn't call to talk about the divorce, Dominick,' she told him softly.

'No?' he came back scathingly. 'It's been four months, Kenzie. Haven't you persuaded Jerome Carlton into proposing yet?'

She flinched at his sarcasm, wondering how she could ever have fooled herself into believing this man was in love with her. But she also had no intention of getting into any sort of slanging match where Jerome Carlton was concerned; Dominick had refused to believe in her innocence four months ago where the other man was concerned, and from his tone of voice now she knew he still didn't believe her.

'I'm still married to you, Dominick,' she reminded him wearily.

'Only just,' he reminded her tersely.

Only just, yes. Once those divorce papers had been signed and witnessed, and there was a legal recognition of their parting, maybe she might be able to once again get on with her life.

Although that idea certainly didn't involve marrying anyone else.

How could she when she had never stopped loving Dominick?

She loved him but knew she was unable to live with

him when he could never feel the same love for her. As his wife she had only ever been an ornament in his well-ordered life, an accessory.

'I need to talk to you properly, Dominick, and I can't do it over the telephone—'

'You aren't suggesting the two of us meet?' he snapped, the derision clear in his voice now.

Kenzie sighed, feeling no more eager to see him again than he obviously was her. It would be so painful to see Dominick again and know that he never had loved, and never would love, her in the way she loved him.

But she knew Dominick's reluctance to see her again was vastly different from her own. She represented the one failure he had had in his life. And failure, as she knew only too well, was something Dominick Masters refused to recognize.

In fact, she had been waiting the last four months for some move of retribution on his part for her ever having dared to leave him!

When it hadn't happened she had decided that perhaps his inactivity *was* his retribution, with Dominick quite capable of imagining her apprehension—and relishing the fact!

'I need to see you—to ask you—something,' she amended carefully. Despite their situation, she ached to see him, but not the coldly distant man, the ice man, of their last meeting, the man she could tell, just from the tone of his voice, that he still was. 'I need to—ask a favour, Dominick,' she expanded slightly breathlessly, wincing at the admission.

'From me?' Dominick couldn't keep the surprise from his voice.

He clearly remembered Kenzie assuring him, on the day she walked out of his life, that their marriage was over, and she would never ask him for anything ever again!

Except for a divorce, of course.

His mouth tightened. 'You have a damned nerve thinking that you can just waltz back into my life after four months and ask me for anything—'

'Dominick, please—'

'No—*you* please!' he cut in forcefully. 'You walked out on me, Kenzie. On our marriage. Straight into the arms of another man! And now you want *me* to do *you* a favour?'

'I did not leave you for another man!' she came back just as strongly, knowing he didn't believe her, that he never had, but determined never to stop claiming her innocence.

'I happen to know differently,' Dominick rasped.

'You don't know the first thing about me, Dominick.' She sighed. 'You never did.'

The first shock of hearing from her had passed now, her conversation such that Dominick was pretty sure this call was just a coincidence. After all, Kenzie had no idea that the sword of Damocles—a blow entirely of Dominick's devising!—was about to drop on her lover's head.

'I'm not—the favour I have to ask isn't for me, Dominick,' she came back sharply. 'Well…not really,' she amended impatiently. 'Maybe,' she muttered uncomfortably.

'Perhaps you had better let me be the judge of that, Kenzie,' he decided tersely. 'Tell me what it is you— need, from me—' he used the word deliberately '—and I'll tell you if I'm willing to give it.'

'Not over the telephone,' she insisted determinedly. 'I need to explain a few things to you first, to help you understand—Dominick, could you meet me for lunch?'

His brows rose at the suggestion. Talking to her on the telephone was one thing, but actually seeing her again, being close to her long-legged beauty, was something else. 'Today?'

'Well, of course—' She broke off her impatient response. 'Yes, today,' she resumed more reasonably. 'If that's possible,' she added abruptly.

Dominick looked at the open diary on his desk-top, unnecessarily so, already knowing that he was free for lunch today.

'I'm afraid it isn't,' he told Kenzie smoothly, totally ignoring the blank space in his diary. 'But I am having dinner at Rimini's at eight o'clock this evening, if you would care to join me there?'

Kenzie winced her dismay at the thought of having dinner with Dominick, tonight or any other time. It meant none of the informality of a crowded lunchtime restaurant that she had been going to suggest, but instead dinner at one of the exclusive restaurants that they had quite often gone to together as husband and wife...

'Couldn't I just meet you for a drink in a bar or something before you go on to dinner?' she suggested, frowning. 'What I have to ask will only take a few minutes, and—'

'Scared, Kenzie?' Dominick interrupted tauntingly.

She bristled. 'Of you? Hardly!' she dismissed scathingly, knowing that wasn't quite true. Although she wasn't scared of Dominick himself, she knew that, with his wealth and power, the sort of retribution he was capable of could be immense! 'I just don't see the point of completely ruining both our evenings, that's all.'

'Just mine, hmm?' he mused scornfully. 'You're the one that asked for this meeting, Kenzie, not me,' he reminded her. 'In the circumstances, I believe I'm allowed to set the terms for that meeting. In which case, it's dinner this evening or nothing,' he stated.

She'd had a feeling he was going to say that!

'Then I suppose I will have to agree to that, won't I?' she snapped, the hours, instead of minutes, she would now have to spend in Dominick's company looming before her like a deep, dark chasm.

'Don't sound too eager, Kenzie,' he taunted. 'I might get the wrong idea.'

'I wouldn't if I were you!' she came back tartly. 'Nothing has changed. I just need to talk to you, that's all,' she added huskily.

'It must be something really big, Kenzie, if you're willing to see me again,' he mused, finding himself smiling at Kenzie's obvious frustration with the situation.

It was the sort of relaxed smile he hadn't given for months. Four months, in fact. Since Kenzie had left him…

His smile evaporated as quickly as it had appeared.

Kenzie had left him, had walked out on their marriage, because, she had claimed, he was incapable of feeling the love for her that she had for him, and after only nine months of being married she simply couldn't live with him any more.

But her claims that it had been his lack of love for her that had ended their marriage had all been a lie, a fabrication, in an effort to hide the affair she was embroiled in with Jerome Carlton.

He sobered completely at the thought of the other man in Kenzie's life, and in her bed. He knew that, despite all the things she had said about the fidelity of love and marriage, she had been involved with another man for weeks before their marriage had finally come to its bitter end!

But now, it seemed, she wanted something from him, a favour, she said.

The retribution he had planned was for Jerome Carlton alone, but he knew that the shock waves of the other man's fall from power would ultimately shatter Kenzie's world too.

But now Kenzie had brought herself willingly back into his life.

It was like the spider and the fly…

CHAPTER TWO

KENZIE had no idea what she was doing sitting in a restaurant waiting to have dinner with Dominick Masters, her almost ex-husband.

He was late.

Deliberately so, she was sure, in an effort to unnerve her.

As if she didn't feel nervous enough about this meeting already!

A fact Dominick would be well aware of. Just as he had to be aware that any situation serious enough for her to have the need to call him in the first place had to be such that she couldn't just walk out of here before he deigned to arrived.

Which was why, she was sure, he was purposely keeping her waiting.

Much to the interest of the other diners, not that they expressed it overtly. The face of Kenzie Miller was well known from her catwalk days, and more recently from the advertisements she appeared in on worldwide television as well as billboards and promotions in stores. Kenzie Miller, the face of Carlton Cosmetics.

Kenzie Miller, international model, sitting on her own for the last fifteen minutes at a table set for two, obviously having been stood up by her date for the evening!

No doubt this was Dominick's idea of a joke, a minor vengeance for her having walked out on him, but, favour or no favour, if he didn't turn up in the next three minutes she was walking out of here—

He had just walked into the restaurant!

Even if she hadn't seen him enter Kenzie would have known of his arrival. She could feel the familiar ripple of awareness down her spine at his proximity, and the warmth of her breasts as they began to tingle, while an even hotter fire began in the pit of her stomach.

It hadn't gone away then, her complete physical awareness of Dominick.

Not that she had ever thought that it would.

It was just distressing to once again be confronted with the proof. He looked amazing, Kenzie acknowledged, in his dark tailored suit and white silk shirt. She imagined the long muscular length of his powerful body underneath, and watched his dark hair as his head moved, hair that she remembered burying her fingers in as she drew his head down to hers and…

He wasn't even looking her way, damn him. She watched him looking perfectly relaxed as he paused to talk to the *maître d'*.

Her stomach felt as if it were churned up into knots, and she was suddenly struck by the enormity of what she was doing. But what choice did she have?

Really?

None.

Dominick was walking over to their table now, acknowledging several acquaintances along the way, seemingly completely unaware of her presence. Or that he was almost twenty minutes late!

'I hope I haven't kept you waiting,' he said coolly as he took his seat opposite hers at the table, looking just as devastatingly handsome as he always had. As devastatingly handsome as she had imagined while talking to him on the telephone earlier today. 'I was—unavoidably detained,' he drawled.

Dominick had seen Kenzie as soon as he'd entered the restaurant, and had been shocked how just looking at her could still render him momentarily speechless. His mouth had gone dry, and he had deliberately paused to talk to the *maître d'* in order to give himself time to get over his initial response.

Kenzie looked beautiful this evening. Stunningly so, with her long dark hair loose down her spine, the figure-hugging green strapless dress she wore revealing bare satin shoulders and the creamy swell of her breasts. The dress was an exact match in colour for the emerald of her eyes, eyes surrounded by the darkest, longest lashes Dominick had ever seen, and her full lips held the promise of a passion he had come to know intimately.

But Kenzie wasn't just beautiful; she had something else, a grace, an inborn sensuality that was apparent even in stillness, like now.

The first time he had looked at her he had felt as if someone had punched him in the solar plexus. Today, under totally different circumstances, he felt the same painful blow as he studied her beneath hooded lids.

None of that emotion showed in the harsh arrogance of his face as he looked across at her. 'You're looking well, Kenzie,' he told her distantly as he nodded his thanks to the wine waiter who was pouring two glasses of the wine Dominick always ordered when dining here. 'Obviously taking a lover suits you,' he added harshly.

'Letting your overactive imagination run away with you again, Dominick?' she bit out tartly, firmly pushing away her awareness of him as she tossed the long length of her hair back over her bare shoulders to meet his gaze firmly.

She had dressed carefully for their meeting this evening, choosing to wear her hair down the way she knew Dominick preferred it, and a clinging green dress that showed off the perfection of her figure.

She was going to need every weapon she could find to withstand the scorn Dominick now felt for her, and she had decided that she wouldn't try to detract from the beauty of the face and figure with which she had made her fortune, but emphasize them instead. If only to show Dominick what he had given up when he had chosen to let her walk away rather than sitting down with her and sorting out their differences.

But the coldness of his dark gaze, as it moved slowly from the top of her head to the slenderness of her waist, didn't show any regret for that loss!

Twenty-seven and a successful model for the last eight years, she never had been able to withstand the coldly analytical gaze that gave away none of Dominick's thoughts or emotions.

If he had any emotions.

Besides physical desire, that was.

She had certainly never seen love shining in those dark depths, not for her or anyone else.

'I prefer not to imagine anything where you and Jerome Carlton are concerned,' he snapped now as he picked up his glass to take a sip of his white wine. 'I was merely stating that the demise of our marriage doesn't seem to have affected your beauty!'

'Oh, let's be precise,' Kenzie muttered with inward resentment for his cool control. If Dominick had seen her a month ago as she had sat for hours by her father's bedside at the hospital, just willing him to live, then he would have seen that she didn't always look beautiful, that sometimes she just looked emotionally distraught.

'Fine,' she dismissed tersely. 'If I could just explain to you why I need to talk to you—'

'I would like to order my food first, if that's okay?' he cut in with smooth determination, his tone of voice telling her it wasn't a question at all but a statement of intent.

He might have left her with no choice but to agree to meet him here at the restaurant, but she really didn't think she could actually *eat* anything. Seeing him again, realizing she still loved him as much as she ever had, and knowing there was no return of love for her in his cold, unemotional gaze, was tearing her apart.

She swallowed hard. 'Go ahead. I won't, if you don't mind.' She closed the menu she had been given without even looking at it, her dark lashes sweeping low over the paleness of her cheeks.

Dominick studied her silently for several seconds, knowing Kenzie had never been one of those models that had to starve herself to stay thin, that her slenderness was as natural as her beauty.

He reached out to cup her chin in his hand and lift her face so that, unless she actually closed her lids completely, her gaze had to meet his.

She had become more adept at hiding her emotions in the last four months, he realized as she easily withstood his searching look.

Yet as he continued to study her he could see very slight changes in her. There was a strain in her green eyes, her face seemed pale beneath her make-up, and her slenderness, now that he had the time to look more closely, bordered on fragile.

'What's happened, Kenzie?' he demanded as he released her chin to sit back in his seat. 'Surely Jerome Carlton hasn't failed to live up to your exacting expectations, too?' he scorned.

She gave a weary sigh. 'Why haven't you ever believed me when I tell you I have never been involved with Jerome on a personal level?' She shook her head.

Why? Because Dominick knew exactly how the other man had pursued her five months ago, desperate to get Kenzie as the 'face' for his company's new line in beauty products.

And with the chasm that had recently developed in their marriage, Dominick knew it had been all too easy for Jerome Carlton to seduce Kenzie, and to persuade her into being a part of his life as well as contracted to his company.

He knew all these things because Jerome Carlton had personally taken delight in relating them to him!

'Where does Jerome think you are this evening?' he challenged. 'Not out to dinner with me, I'm sure?' he taunted.

She drew in a sharp breath before releasing it in a sigh. 'I haven't come here to discuss Jerome with you. I—actually I haven't seen him for several weeks. My father has been ill, you see, and—'

'Donald has?' Dominick echoed sharply, waving away the waiter who came to take their food order, too interested in what Kenzie was saying to even think about food. Especially the part where she said she hadn't seen Jerome for several weeks…

He also wanted to hear more about Donald. He had only found the time to meet the older man three times during his marriage to Kenzie, but he had liked him and had to admire the easy way he had survived being the only male member of a household dominated by his wife and four daughters.

Kenzie swallowed hard. 'He wasn't feeling well for some months, and then a month ago he had a heart attack—'

'Why the hell didn't you let me know?' Dominick questioned immediately.

She blinked across at him in surprise. As she had learnt to her cost, Dominick didn't 'do' family. Coming from a family that had been split apart when he was only eight, and then presented with a series of stepmothers and stepfathers, he could perhaps have welcomed the close-knit family Kenzie had brought into their marriage. But he hadn't, he didn't trust or want a family, and had kept his emotional as well as physical distance from all of them.

And only his emotional distance from Kenzie, she remembered achingly.

'Why on earth would I do that?' she prompted incredulously. 'You never showed any interest in my family when we were married, so why would you want to be bothered now that we're divorced?'

'Separated,' Dominick corrected harshly. 'I haven't signed the divorce papers yet,' he reminded her.

No, he hadn't, although Kenzie didn't understand why not. She had thought he would be glad to get rid of her and the marriage he wished had never happened. But weeks after they had been sent, as far as she knew the papers remained unsigned as well as unreturned.

In the circumstances, perhaps that was as well...

It certainly made it a little easier to come here and talk to him this evening. A little...

'A technicality,' she accepted heavily. 'I—' She broke off as a waiter put a plate of hors d'oeuvres in the centre of the table before making a discreet exit.

Dominick turned to give the waiter a rueful smile, appreciative of the fact that the other man had realized the tension bouncing off this table meant there would be no meal ordered here this evening. Or perhaps he was just another person who found Kenzie's ethereal beauty enthralling...

Kenzie seemed to have been momentarily knocked off balance too. 'How are your own parents?' she prompted awkwardly.

He gave a rueful shake of his head. Kenzie had met both his parents only once, separately of course, in which meetings his father had been leeringly flirtatious and his mother had been interested in learning what beauty products Kenzie used to maintain her natural loveliness.

Kenzie had dealt with those meetings with teasing laughter for his father, and warm interest for his mother.

She had impressed Dominick at the time, he grudg-ingly acknowledged, particularly considering that neither of his parents had been overly interested in his marriage, even when he had told them he and Kenzie had separated.

'The same,' he answered dismissively. 'And stop trying to change the subject, Kenzie. Tell me about your father.'

She absently picked up a prawn confection from the plate and popped it into her mouth before answering him.

Dominick found his attention caught by the fullness of her lips, lips that he had kissed, lips that had kissed him and pleasured him to new heights.

God, how he still wanted her!

And how dearly he wished that he didn't…!

Her tongue moved to moisten those lips now, her gaze once again shadowed. 'He had a heart attack,' she repeated evenly.

Dominick knew what a blow that must have been for the Miller women, for Nancy, his wife of thirty years, for the youngest daughter Kathy, for Carly and Suzie, and for the eldest daughter, Kenzie. Donald was adored by all of them.

The eldest daughter Kenzie… Who had once been Dominick's wife. Who had come to him now to ask for his help in some way, albeit reluctantly. But what help could he possibly be to her? Kenzie was extremely rich in her own right, and could afford to give her father the best medical care available, so what could Dominick possibly give her that she didn't already have?

Kenzie knew it was time to stop prevaricating, that Dominick would either help her or he wouldn't. It was better to know sooner rather than later.

She drew in a deep breath. 'My sister Kathy is going

to be married on Saturday. Kathy wanted to cancel the wedding until my father is feeling better, but he's adamant that those arrangements not be changed.'

Dominick frowned. 'And you want me to send her a wedding gift…?'

'No, of course not,' she sighed impatiently; if only it were that simple!

'You surely don't want me to give Kathy away in your father's stead?' he taunted.

'You're being ridiculous now!' Kenzie said, exasperated. 'What I want, what I need from you— This isn't easy for me, Dominick!' She groaned, her eyes, those incredible green eyes, filled with tears now.

He gave a shake of his head, his brown gaze guarded. 'I'm afraid I can't help you there,' he rasped.

No, he couldn't, could he?

During the months they had been apart Kenzie had had plenty of time to realize that it wasn't completely Dominick's fault that their marriage had been such a disaster.

He had never lied to her, having always been completely honest about his feelings for her, and had never once, either before or after they were married, said that he was in love with her, or that it was ever more than her body that held him in thrall. It had only been her own deep love for him, she had come to realize, her romantic ideal of what marriage should be, that had convinced her otherwise.

Until faced, irrevocably, with the painful truth…

She swallowed hard. 'The thing is—Dominick, what I do need is for you—for you to come to Kathy's wedding with me on Saturday!' She looked up at him now, needing to see his reaction.

To say he was stunned was an understatement, although he quickly masked the emotion, his gaze once again narrowing, questioningly now. And all the time his razor-sharp brain was working behind his guarded appearance, evaluating, assessing.

But this time not reaching a logical conclusion…

Dominick gave a shake of his head. 'Why?' he prompted economically.

This was so like Dominick. Blunt. To the point.

And it would be better if Kenzie answered him in the same way. 'Because they all expect you to be there!'

'Why?' he repeated tautly.

'Because—because I've never told my family that we're separated!' The words came out in a rush, her face once again pale as she looked at Dominick.

Dominick frowned. Kenzie's family didn't *know* their marriage was over, that it had been so for four months?

The newspapers, thankfully, didn't seem to have picked up on the rift in the marriage yet. The fact that both of them often travelled abroad, necessitating lengthy partings, probably accounted for that. But why hadn't Kenzie told her family at least?

What possible reason could she have for not telling them?

Considering Kenzie had left him to go to another man this oversight didn't make a lot of sense to him.

Her father had had his heart attack a month ago, Kenzie had said, which was before or after she'd had the divorce papers sent to Dominick?

After, he would hazard a guess, otherwise she would surely have told her family the truth by now.

Kenzie couldn't meet the intensity of Dominick's

gaze now, knowing that not telling her family of their estrangement was stupid, and that her hope that their separation wouldn't last had been even sillier.

But for weeks she *had* hoped. She had simply refused to believe that Dominick couldn't return at least some of the love she felt for him, and that once they were apart he would come to realize how much he really did love her. She also hoped he would acknowledge that his accusations concerning her sexual involvement with Jerome Carlton were completely untrue.

It was because she had longed for a reconciliation, that she had decided there was no reason to tell her family of the estrangement yet.

It hadn't been all that difficult to keep it from them either. She had been away in America for almost a month after she and Dominick had parted, and redirecting her mail, using her mobile whenever she called them, had been an easy way of concealing her change of address. None of her family had questioned why Dominick wasn't with her when she'd visited, her family knowing how busy he was and how much he travelled on business. Her explanation that he was in Australia when her father had become ill had been easily accepted by all of them.

But she had waited in vain for Dominick to realize he cared for her after all, even the serving of the divorce papers eliciting no response from him, at which point she had had no choice but to accept that he really had never loved her, and that their marriage really was over.

Which was when she had known she had no choice but to tell her family the truth.

But before she had been able to do so her father had

had his heart attack, and for the last month she had forgotten everything but willing him to get better.

Which he had. And the doctors were hopeful that, with time, and no undue stress, he would make a full recovery.

In the meantime, her sister's wedding was on Saturday, and her family still had no idea that she and Dominick were no longer together.

No undue stress, the doctors had said her father needed.

It was definitely not the time for him to learn that the marriage of his eldest daughter was going to end in divorce!

Which was why she had no choice but to ask Dominick if, for one day only, he would agree to pose as her husband.

The real question was, would he agree to do it…?

CHAPTER THREE

'WHY didn't you tell them, Kenzie?' Dominick demanded. He hadn't exactly gone around shouting about the failure of their marriage either, but he would have thought Kenzie would have at least told her own family…

She glared at him, tears still in her eyes, precariously balanced on those long, dark lashes. 'And admit what an idiot I had been ever to have thought— Tell them that our marriage had lasted only nine months?' she amended with a self-derisive shake of her head. 'I was going to tell them—I had every intention of telling them—but everyone was so wrapped up in the plans for Kathy's wedding! And then Carly announced that she's expecting a baby, closely followed by Suzie announcing she was too. And I couldn't—I just couldn't—'

'Kenzie—'

'Don't!' She glared across the table at him, her face very pale. 'You made your feelings about "bringing children into this world" perfectly clear five months ago!'

The question of children had never arisen when they had been just seeing each other, and when they had been newly married—a constant source of amazement to the jaded Dominick!—he had given little thought to the subject, either. So it had come as a complete surprise to him after they had been married for eight months that Kenzie had brought up the idea of them having a baby together.

Kenzie had seemed to draw away from him after his refusal to even contemplate the thought, and soon she had been no longer the fiery lover and the laughing companion of their first months of marriage. Then she had come to him a month later and told him she had decided to take up Jerome Carlton's offer to work exclusively for Carlton Cosmetics, and that she was leaving for America the following week.

At which point Dominick had probably made the biggest mistake of his life, by issuing the ultimatum that if Kenzie left she needn't bother coming back…!

Not only had she left, but Jerome Carlton had been standing smugly at her side when she had!

Carlton Cosmetics, Dominick now knew, was a family run company, Jack Carlton having retired several years ago to leave the running of the business to his eldest son Jerome. There was also a younger brother and sister, Adrian and Caroline, who were significant shareholders.

Dominick knew this because over the course of the last four months he had made it his business to know!

'I—you do see my problem, Dominick?' Kenzie looked at him anxiously.

'Oh, I see your problem, all right, Kenzie,' he admitted coldly. 'In the circumstances, it wouldn't do at all to turn up at Kathy's wedding with your lover in tow, now would it?'

Kenzie could feel herself trembling now. 'That was

never an option,' she told him flatly. 'I do intend telling my family the truth, Dominick, I—just not now. So...' she breathed deeply, her gaze challenging '...will you come to the wedding with me on Saturday or not? For my father's sake, if nothing else,' she added persuasively.

'That's emotional blackmail, Kenzie, and you damn well know it!' he replied harshly.

Was it? Probably. But it wasn't for her own personal gain; it was only to help her father.

Although it was obvious Dominick didn't see it that way!

'I know it's a lot to ask, and I really wouldn't have bothered if I didn't think it was important. I would be very grateful if you would do this for me, Dominick,' she added quietly.

If anything his expression became even colder, his eyes so dark now the black of the iris wasn't distinguishable from the brown. 'Tell me if I'm mistaken, Kenzie,' he murmured, scowling darkly, 'but it sounds very much to me as if you're offering yourself up to me as some sort of human sacrifice in order to coerce me into agreeing to be your husband again for a day?'

'Of course I'm not!' She gasped, staring at him incredulously. 'I didn't mean— That wasn't what I meant at all— Oh, this is hopeless!' She threw up her hands in frustrated anger. 'Forget I asked! Forget I even told you any of this! I'll find some other way of solving the problem!' she added determinedly.

Dominick looked at her long, slender hands, the hands that used to touch and caress him...

Hands that he knew had been touching and caressing another man for the last five months!

It was obvious now why Kenzie hadn't seen Jerome Carlton for several weeks—she could hardly drag her lover along to visit her father in hospital when her family weren't even aware she *had* a lover!

'What are you going to do, Kenzie, tell them that I'm too tied up on business to attend Kathy's wedding?' he scorned.

She had already tried that. Last weekend when she had gone home to visit, in fact. To which her father had assured her that of course Dominick would be back from his business trip to Australia in time for Kathy's wedding, that he was probably going to surprise her by arriving back unexpectedly.

Something she knew there was no chance of Dominick doing. Ever.

She shook her head impatiently. 'I've already told them you're away in Sydney on business, but my father is absolutely certain that you will make the effort to be back in time to attend your own sister-in-law's wedding.'

'It's nice to know that one member of the family has a little faith in me!' Dominick's expression was bleak and unapproachable.

Kenzie opened her mouth to protest. And then shut it again. What could she possibly say that wouldn't make this situation worse?

'This isn't the place for this conversation,' Dominick told her grimly, picking up his wineglass and throwing the contents to the back of his throat before standing up. 'Let's get out of here,' he muttered, taking her arm as she stood up to join him.

Kenzie forced herself not to tremble as he touched her, determined not to let him see how he still affected her.

Dominick kept his hand lightly under her elbow as they made their way through the crowded tables, nodding his thanks to the maître d' as he passed. He had an account with the restaurant, and he would make sure he tipped the man very generously when he settled the bill at the end of the month.

'Where are we going?' Kenzie prompted stiffly once Dominick had flagged down a cab, very aware of the light brush of his hand against her spine now.

'My apartment,' he bit out dryly.

Kenzie held back from getting inside the cab. 'Your—the apartment where you—where we—'

'Lived after we were married?' he finished coldly. 'But of course that apartment, Kenzie. It's been my English home for over five years; why would I have bothered to move?'

Why indeed? Kenzie accepted heavily as she got into the back of the taxi, shooting over to the far side of the seat so that not even their thighs could come into accidental contact.

Dominick, she had discovered during their nine months of marriage, didn't particularly like change, and, for all that he had business dealings all over the world, he had homes in all those countries too, apartments that were always kept ready for his use, disliking intensely the need to stay in hotels. Even his own.

Kenzie had put this need down to the fact that his childhood had been so erratic, no one place ever really becoming home as he'd ping-ponged between his parents' houses after their divorce. His mother had retained the family home, but had moved in a constant stream of husbands and lovers, while his father, after an unsuccessful second marriage, had entertained various women in his city apartment.

She didn't relish the idea of going to Dominick's apartment, the home she had shared with him as his wife, as she remembered all too clearly the intimacies they had shared there, as well as that last terrible scene before she had left him.

She might not like it, but, until Dominick had said a definite no about accompanying her to the wedding on Saturday, she was willing to continue this conversation wherever Dominick decided.

At least he was still listening to her.

'Drink?' he offered once they were in the apartment, holding up the brandy decanter before pouring a measure of the dark gold liquid into a glass.

Would brandy make any difference to the trepidation she felt? she wondered ruefully. Probably not, but it might help to calm her nerves a little. 'Yes. Thank you,' she accepted as he handed her the glass before pouring another one for himself.

Dominick watched the slender arch of her throat as she took a swallow of the brandy, the creamy softness of her skin, while at the same time inwardly acknowledging that he had missed her in his life this last few months, and not just in his bed. Sometimes he had ached with wanting her to talk to, to laugh with.

'So—' his voice was harsher than ever as he determinedly squashed down his thoughts '—I believe we were discussing what sacrifice you're willing to make in order to persuade me to accompany you to Kathy's wedding on Saturday…?'

Kenzie had been about to swallow another sip of

brandy, but instead gasped at the outrageousness of Dominick's remark, gulping too quickly in the process, and starting to cough as the fiery liquid took her breath away.

'Careful!' Dominick moved to pat her on the back.

A little too enthusiastically, as far as Kenzie was concerned; she was sure there was no need for him to be quite so heavy-handed!

'You did that on purpose!' she told him fiercely once she could speak, her cheeks red, and her eyes glowing deeply green with anger.

'More brandy?' he offered wryly as he took the empty glass from her unresisting fingers.

'No, thank you,' she snapped. 'This was a mistake—'

'How do you know that when I haven't even given you my answer yet?' he challenged huskily.

She shook her head. 'You're just playing with me, Dominick. You're taking some sort of perverted pleasure in making me squirm, when all the time you know you're going to say no—'

'I don't know that,' he cut in softly. 'And neither do you,' he added.

Kenzie sighed in frustration. 'I don't know why I ever thought appealing to your better nature would work—'

'Considering we both know I don't *have* a better nature?'

Dominick put in scornfully.

That wasn't true. Dominick had his faults, but she could never have fallen in love with him if he didn't have a softer, more charming side to him.

But being with him again now she realized what a fool she had been to ever hope that Dominick would want her back, and to believe that she was the one woman that Dominick could love, when it was obvious he had never been in love before. Yes, she had been a fool. A silly, romantic fool.

And she hadn't seen that softer, more charming side to him since that day, four months ago, when she had told him she had decided to accept the offer from Carlton Cosmetics, an offer that would take her to America for a month.

They had been going through a difficult patch in their marriage, and she had thought that month apart would give them a breathing space away from each other, for them both to sit and reflect, and perhaps to come to some sort of compromise concerning their differences over the subject of having children.

Instead Dominick had accused her of being involved with Jerome Carlton personally rather than just his company, of having an affair with the other man, refusing to believe her denials.

'You weren't sarcastic and hurtful like this when we met, Dominick.' She gave a pained frown.

'Maybe I was just being charming then because I wanted to get you into bed?' he derided. 'Or maybe it's just that having your wife leave you for the bed of another man has this effect on you! Tell me, Kenzie, is he a good lover?' He studied her between narrowed lids. 'A better lover than me?'

Just the thought of Kenzie in the arms of the charismatically handsome Jerome Carlton had driven Dominick to say things, do things, he might otherwise not have done. But having said them, there had been no going back.

The arrival of the divorce papers three months after their separation only confirmed her intention to marry the other man as far as Dominick was concerned.

'I hope he found me a satisfactory teacher!' Dominick bit out harshly at her continued silence at his taunt, determinedly ignoring the way her cheeks had paled at his words.

He still couldn't bear the thought of any other man touching her and caressing her in the way he liked to.

Was he going insane? He groaned inwardly as he turned away abruptly. Had seeing Kenzie again driven him over the edge of some precipice he had been fighting against for the last four months as he had considered his plans of retribution?

That had to be it.

There could be no other explanation for the jealousy he felt.

'Look, Dominick.' She spoke woodenly. 'Other than continuing to assure you that Jerome and I have never been lovers, not when the two of us were married, or since, I don't have any other way of convincing you that you are completely wrong about my involvement with him!'

Assurances that were a complete waste of time when her lover had no such qualms about acknowledging their involvement!

Besides, it was too late for that. It had been too late the very first moment Kenzie had responded to Jerome Carlton's seduction.

Dominick had believed that Kenzie's lack of physical involvement with men before their marriage meant that the least he could expect from her was fidelity. Knowing of her affair with Jerome Carlton just made her as untrustworthy as every other woman, including his own mother, he had ever been close to.

'I think perhaps I should leave now, Dominick,' Kenzie said softly. 'Before this conversation becomes any more insulting!'

They were deliberately hurting each other, he knew, and he forced the tension to leave his shoulders as he turned back to face her, coming to his decision. 'What time is Kathy's wedding on Saturday?' he prompted abruptly.

Kenzie's eyes widened. 'Why do you want to know…?' she asked warily.

Dominick's mouth twisted derisively. 'It's hardly going to serve its purpose if I arrive too late for the wedding, now, is it?'

He was going to help her out, after all? He was going to help her protect her father from the truth, in this charade that she should have ended long ago and now couldn't find the right words, or time, in which to do so?

She swallowed hard. 'If you're serious—if you're really willing to do this—my parents are expecting us both down for a family dinner on Friday evening,' she told him, frowning.

'Kenzie, you said you wanted me to accompany you to the wedding, and presumably you would expect me to stay on for the reception afterwards. Isn't wanting me to go to your parents' home on the Friday evening, as well, a little above and beyond…?' he mocked scathingly.

She grimaced. 'It's worse than that, I'm afraid; we're expected to stay overnight at my parents' house on the Friday evening, too.'

Which, if Dominick agreed, she had already known was going to be something of a problem. Although not an insurmountable one. All three of her parents' guest bedrooms had twin beds, so they wouldn't actually be sharing a bed, just the room.

Although Dominick's cool control, and her own quivering response just to the touch of his hand on her arm and back, said *she* was the one in more danger of finding their proximity overwhelming...

Dominick continued to look at her for several long seconds, his expression guarded as he took in her silken hair, before his gaze shifted slightly to her face, and then he wished it hadn't as he felt almost as if he were drowning in the depths of her eyes, those incredible, emerald-coloured eyes.

Deceptively honest eyes, he reminded himself with cold determination, thinking of how she continued to lie about her involvement with Jerome.

But now Kenzie was here, however briefly, and was willingly, if unwittingly, putting herself back in his power...

'I'm sure staying over won't be a problem, Kenzie,' he accepted dismissively.

She eyed him thoughtfully, at last seeming to realize something of what she was doing. 'It won't?'

'Not at all,' he drawled with satisfaction. 'We shared a bed for nine months, I'm sure we can share a bedroom again for a single night only.'

Kenzie felt knocked slightly off balance by his sudden acquiescence, as she had been sure she would have to do some more quick talking once Dominick knew the full extent of the commitment she was asking him to make.

'I—fine,' she accepted awkwardly, too relieved right

now that he had agreed to come to the wedding with her to want to stand and dissect his response. No doubt she would have plenty of time to reflect on that later! All that was important at the moment was her father's continuing peace of mind. 'We're expected in Worcestershire for about seven o'clock…'

'I'll drive us there.' He nodded. 'Does a four o'clock departure suit you?'

'Perfect.' She nodded, still frowning, but unable to read any of Dominick's own thoughts from his deliberately closed expression.

'My address in London is—'

'I know your address, Kenzie,' he cut in disparagingly.

He knew where she lived…? He knew of the apartment she had bought and moved into when she'd returned from the States?

'It was on the divorce papers,' Dominick reminded her grimly, all teasing gone now. 'Now, if you wouldn't mind…?' he added tersely. 'I've already wasted enough time on this subject this evening. I have some work I need to do.'

Her creamy brow cleared of its frown as she gave a derisive smile. 'Of course you do,' she accepted ruefully, turning to leave.

'Oh, and, Kenzie…?' He stopped her before she had taken two steps.

She turned back slowly, warily. 'Yes…?'

His mouth twisted mockingly. 'I'll let you know what I want in return for—helping you out, in this way.'

Kenzie felt the colour drain from her cheeks. 'What *you* want in return…?' she repeated carefully.

'Of course,' Dominick replied. 'You didn't seriously

think I was going to inconvenience myself in this way for nothing?'

She hadn't had any thoughts at all beyond getting him to agree to come to the wedding on Saturday!

He shook his head as he stared at her. 'How naïve you still are, Kenzie,' he taunted. 'I'll give it some thought in the next few days and let you know what I decide is an appropriate payment.'

And until then she would have to be satisfied, Kenzie accepted wearily as she collected her clutch bag from the table in the hallway and let herself into the lift. She didn't doubt that the payment Dominick would extract from her would be something she didn't want to give.

Or worse, it would be something she *did* want to give, but would be opening herself up to all sorts of pain if she did so!

CHAPTER FOUR

'CHEER up, Kenzie,' Dominick said, turning in his car seat to look at her, having parked his black Ferrari in the driveway behind her father's more sedate Mercedes. 'For God's sake, smile!' he added impatiently. Instead of appearing excited and happy to be home for her sister's wedding, Kenzie had the look of a prisoner about to be taken to the gallows. 'I'm willing to do my part to convince your family that we're still a happily married couple, but I'm going to be wasting my time if you continue to look like a whipped puppy!' He scowled.

Heaven knew he was already finding this much more difficult than he had thought it was going to be.

He had viewed with cool detachment several photographs of Kenzie in magazines or on billboards the last four months—it was impossible not to see photographs of her when she was the face of the moment!—but those photographs had been studied perfection, and, while showing a beautiful woman, also gave her an air of untouchability.

He had forgotten just how sexy she looked with her hair wild down her back, and wearing the minimum of make-up. She was dressed in a tight white tee shirt, and faded jeans that fitted low down on her slender hips, their fashionable raggedness only adding to the air of sensuality around her.

An air he had been very much aware of as she sat beside him in the car on the two-hour drive they had just taken together!

Not that he had any intention of letting Kenzie see how much her appearance affected him, talking to her only when necessary, and then only tersely as he'd asked to be reminded of the directions to her parents' home.

'Sorry.' Kenzie grimaced in apology now for her air of preoccupation. 'I was miles away,' she added, knowing by the way Dominick's expression tightened that he wasn't pleased at being told this.

No doubt he imagined she was thinking about her supposed lover, Jerome, and that she was eager to have this weekend over so that she could return to the other man's arms!

The truth was she could think of nothing but Dominick, of how aware she was of him, of how just being with him again like this set her senses tingling.

No doubt Dominick would be extremely amused if he knew how his close proximity had been disturbing her the last two hours, the black tee shirt and faded jeans he wore giving him a much more approachable air—a sexually approachable air!—than his usual formal business suits.

She also couldn't stop thinking, as she hadn't been able to the last couple of days, of what he was going to demand from her in return for being here with her this weekend.

She wondered when he intended exacting that payment!

Dominick gave her one last impatient glance before getting out of the car, having already taken their bags and put them down on the driveway by the time he opened Kenzie's car door and she scrambled out to join him.

'Dominick…?' She put her hand on his arm to stop him picking the bags back up and striding towards the house.

He looked down pointedly at her hand touching his arm. 'What?'

Her mouth twisted ruefully as she let her hand fall back to her side, aware of a slight tingling in her palm just from their brief contact. 'You're right; neither of us exactly has the look of a happily married couple!'

Dominick smoothed his overlong hair back with impatient fingers. 'I'm not sure I know how that's supposed to look!'

Kenzie frowned. 'Maybe if you could just try looking a little less—remote—'

'A little less remote…' he echoed thoughtfully, a look of intent suddenly crossing her face.

Kenzie's eyes widened as she saw that look, taking a slight step backwards. 'Dominick—' She didn't get very far before Dominick took a firm grasp of her arms and pulled her in tight against him, making her aware of every hard muscle and sinew of his body before his head lowered and his lips captured hers to kiss her.

Thoroughly.

Punishingly.

Passionately!

After his uncommunicative silence on the drive up here this was the last thing that Kenzie had been expecting, and she was too surprised to do anything more than grasp the width of his shoulders for support as her lips parted beneath his and his mouth continued to plunder hers.

At last he raised his head to look down at her, dark gaze triumphant as he did so. 'Better?' he taunted huskily.

Much better.

Too much better.

She didn't like that look of victory in his eyes, either, and moved quickly away from him as she pulled out of his arms. 'I don't think there was any need for you to go that far—'

'Weddings always have this effect on me too!' her father interrupted cheerfully as he strolled down the driveway to join them.

'We'll discuss this later,' Kenzie muttered softly.

'Maybe,' Dominick murmured softly, his arm about Kenzie's shoulders as they turned to look at Donald.

And so the pretence began, Kenzie acknowledged agonisingly…

She gave a light laugh as she turned to greet her father, the move effectively taking her out of Dominick's reach.

Dominick stood silently as father and daughter hugged, able to see an unfamiliar fragility to Donald Miller. There was a slight greyness to his face that spoke of recent illness, and his clothes were a little loose on him where he had lost weight.

But the older man's handshake had been firm enough when he had greeted Dominick, and his green eyes warm and welcoming, so unlike his eldest daughter's had been when Dominick had called at her apartment to collect her a couple of hours ago.

'It's good to see you again, Dominick,' Donald told him with genuine pleasure.

'Sir,' he replied with studied politeness; he had never got particularly close to Kenzie's family, and he certainly didn't intend doing so now, either! 'I'm only sorry that work commitments have prevented me from coming to see you before.'

'Oh, we know how busy you are. Besides, I'm perfectly fine now,' Donald dismissed with a wave of his hand. 'Come inside and say hello to Nancy. She'll be so pleased you're here.'

Kenzie's family, Dominick had learnt on being introduced to them, was nothing like his own dysfunctional one. Donald and Nancy, despite having been married for thirty years, were obviously still deeply in love with each other, and their four daughters were also wrapped unpossessively in that closeness.

The hug Nancy gave him, her real pleasure in seeing him again, was also in sharp contrast to the stiffness and suspicion with which Dominick always greeted visits from his own parents. The Millers' obvious genuine warmth in seeing him again didn't sit too comfortably with his decision to take advantage of Kenzie's dilemma and exact revenge on her for ever daring to cheat on him.

Kenzie's sisters Kathy, Carly and Suzie, the latter both in varying stages of pregnancy, hugged him just as happily, while the two middle sisters informed him that their husbands, Colin and Neil, hadn't returned from work yet but would be along later.

The four Miller sisters all shared an incredible dark-haired, green-eyed beauty, and it was overwhelming when confronted with all four of them together, Dominick acknowledged. He was relieved when mother and daughters launched into a discussion about the dresses they were wearing for the wedding tomorrow.

'Our cue to beat a hasty retreat, I think,' Donald told him ruefully. 'Dominick and I are just going to take the dog for a walk,' he said, raising his voice so he could be heard over the women's chatter.

His wife turned to give him a knowing look, the startling beauty of her four daughters obviously inherited from her. 'We don't have a dog, Donald,' she told him dryly. 'And you know you aren't allowed to go to the pub, if that's where you're sneaking off to,' she added reprovingly.

'I take exception to the word "sneaking",' her husband teased back. 'And I'm allowed to go in the pub. I just can't have the pint of beer I would like to have while I'm in there!'

'Well, I'm sure Dominick has absolutely no interest in going to the pub…do you, Dominick?' Nancy looked at him enquiringly.

No, he didn't have any interest in going to a pub, or in being alone with Kenzie's father. But neither did he want to stay here to watch Kenzie as she relaxed in the company of her close-knit family.

Kenzie had asked him to do something for her, and he had agreed, and in return she would give him exactly what he wanted. Getting involved in the intimacy of her family was not part of that bargain.

Kenzie had turned to look at him now, the sharpness of her gaze obviously seeing his lack of enthusiasm for any father/son chats that might occur between the two men once they were alone at the local pub.

'How about Dominick and I take our things up to our

room and freshen up first?' She slipped her hand into the crook of his arm even as she smiled brightly at her family. 'You can "walk the dog" just as easily in half an hour or so, can't you, Dad?' she teased.

'Half an hour, an hour, as long as I can escape from this chatter about weddings for a while!' Her father nodded, his grin belying his words.

Kenzie could feel Dominick's tension as they left the room together and walked up the stairs. She knew that he had always found the easy affection of her family slightly overwhelming. And that it was something he wanted no part of.

It was understandable in a man who hadn't grown up in a loving and stable family, but it also made his agreement to come here this weekend all the more surprising. And the payment he would demand more worrying...

'I'm sorry about that.' She grimaced as she sat down on one of the twin beds in the room her mother had told her she and Dominick were to use for the night. 'Do you think you'll be able to stand a whole weekend of it?' She frowned as she looked at him.

'Oh, I think I'll probably survive,' he drawled, thrusting his hands into the pockets of his denims as he moved restlessly around the room. 'What's the prognosis on your father?' he asked as he remembered, despite Donald's cheerfulness, those tell-tale signs of recent illness in the older man.

'Good.' Kenzie nodded, dark lashes fanning down over her cheeks as she looked towards the floor. 'It was more—frightening, than anything else, I think.' She glanced up at him, her eyes bruised and shadowed. 'The doctors say it's a warning for him to slow down, that's all, that he can return to work at his estate agency in a couple of months' time. But my mother wants him to sell up and take early retirement,' she added ruefully, aware that she was talking too much in her nervousness of being alone with Dominick. She was sure he didn't really want to hear all this, and that his interest had just been idle conversation on his part.

Dominick nodded. 'And?'

She shrugged. 'He says he isn't sixty yet, and he hasn't earnt enough money to retire. But they won't accept any help from me,' she added with a sigh.

He could see how Nancy and Donald would baulk at accepting financial security from their eldest daughter. But what—

Damn it, he had no intention of being sucked into this warmly loving family!

It was against every principle of aloof self-containment he had lived his life by since he had been able to completely escape his parents' influence twenty years ago.

Despite having the grades, he had chosen not to go to college, and instead had worked in a hotel, working his way up from lowly Porter to Assistant Manager, and then Manager by the age of only twenty-three. Then he had gone completely out on a limb to finance the buying of the hotel and had completely turned it around into a profit-making concern.

That first hotel had only been the start, and now he owned hotels and apartments all over the world, amongst other things.

Very shortly, when his four months of planning came to fruition, he intended owning a cosmetics company too…

Before, he had managed to achieve what he had because he had never allowed emotions to overrule his head.

Until he had met and married Kenzie…

A chink in his armour.

But a chink, once he'd had her safely installed in his life as his wife, that he had kept under perfect control.

Until she'd begun to question why he never told her he loved her.

Until she'd begun to talk about them having a baby together.

Kenzie had insisted that the child the two of them had together wouldn't experience the emotionally battered upbringing he'd had. But Dominick had remained adamant against that argument, a development that had obviously caused Kenzie deep unhappiness.

As far as Dominick had been concerned though, there had been no reason for them to have children. They had been happy as they were, so why rock the boat?

Kenzie hadn't seen it that way, and things had become incredibly strained between them, with their lovemaking no longer the pleasure it had once been, and a barrier seeming to come down between them.

When Carlton Cosmetics, in the guise of Jerome Carlton himself, had begun to spend a lot of time with her in an effort to persuade her into accepting a lucrative contract to be the face of their new product, that estrangement had deepened.

Quite to what extent Dominick hadn't been made aware of until he'd spoken to Jerome Carlton some weeks later.

And by then it had been too late. Kenzie had made her choice, and it hadn't been him or their marriage.

She had accepted the contract Jerome Carlton had offered on behalf of Carlton Cosmetics—and Carlton's more personal offer that she move into his life!

Kenzie breathed a sigh, and stood up, the movement bringing Dominick's attention away from his thoughts. 'The bathroom is through there.' She pointed to an adjoining door. 'Take as long as you like. Don't come down again at all, if you would rather not. I'm sure my family will accept that you're tired after working all day and then having to drive here.'

'I'm thirty-eight, Kenzie, not eighty-eight!' he rasped impatiently. 'And I seem to remember being perfectly capable of going in to work the next morning as usual after some of our more—strenuous sexual marathons,' he added tauntingly.

Kenzie paused in the doorway, her expression pained. 'And there you have the difference between us in stark reality, Dominick,' she told him sadly. She knew that difference was everything, and that it always had been, only she had been too much in love with Dominick, too blind to see it, at the time. 'You see, I thought the two of us were making love,' she explained at his scowl, 'not having a "sexual marathon"!'

His mouth twisted scathingly. 'You always did like to pretty things up in rose-coloured glasses!'

'Whereas you,' she murmured softly, 'have always worn blinkers and so see nothing at all except what's directly in front of your nose, giving you an extremely narrow view of the world!' She closed the door softly behind her as she left, knowing there was nothing more to be said, and that she couldn't reach Dominick this way. She never had been able to.

She blinked back the tears as she moved hurriedly

back down the stairs to rejoin her family, eager to be back amongst their warmth and love.

Dominick gazed after her with pitying derision.

Love!

That was for people like Kenzie, not him. It was for people who hadn't had the notion of love kicked out of them by their own parents' infidelities when they were a kid. Because loving someone, one person, for a lifetime, simply didn't exist.

But what about Nancy and Donald? an annoying little voice asked inside his head.

An exception, not the rule, he told himself firmly. One successful marriage didn't make up for the fact that almost one in two marriages ended in divorce nowadays.

Love wasn't to be trusted, he had learnt at a very early age. It only made fools of everyone—and he had no intention of ever joining the ranks of the foolish!

CHAPTER FIVE

'WHAT did you and Dad talk about while you were out?' Kenzie prompted curiously as she came back from preparing for bed in the adjoining bathroom.

The two men had disappeared together for over an hour earlier once Dominick had come back downstairs, and Kenzie had been unable to stop feeling anxious the whole time they'd been gone. She wondered what two such different men could possibly have found to discuss for that length of time, and her look of concern had earned her quite a lot of teasing from her sisters as they had mistaken that anxiety for missing Dominick.

Her family obviously had no idea, but she had got used to missing Dominick during their months of separation. She had never quite accepted it, but at the same time she knew there was no point in pulling herself to emotional shreds over something she, and her love, couldn't change. Dominick couldn't ever change.

So she had smiled good-naturedly through her sisters' teasing, the pressure having eased off by the arrival of Colin and Neil, which had been quickly followed by her father and Dominick's return. The nine of them—Kathy's fiancé Derek had been banned from seeing his bride until the wedding tomorrow—had then all sat down to the meal the women had prepared in the men's absence.

Now was the first opportunity this evening Kenzie had had to talk to Dominick privately.

She needed to talk, to cover the awkwardness she felt in coming back to the bedroom wearing only peach-coloured silk pyjamas. Dominick was sprawled out on one of the beds still fully dressed, his gaze hooded as he straightened up on the pillow to look at her.

'Very sexy,' he murmured as he scrutinized her slowly up and down. 'As I recall you always slept naked; how long have you been wearing those passion killers?'

Her eyes glittered angrily. 'Since I knew I had to share a bedroom for the night with my ex-husband!' She had slept naked during their marriage because there had been little point in her wearing anything—Dominick had always thrown it off within minutes of their getting into bed.

'Almost ex-husband,' Dominick corrected grimly, straightening to get a better look at her. 'I haven't decided whether or not to sign the papers yet,' he added distractedly, revising his initial impression of the pyjamas now that he could see the way the silky material fell smoothly over the pertness of Kenzie's breasts. He noticed that her nipples hardened under his gaze.

In arousal.

So she wasn't as sexually immune to him as she wanted him to believe, after all...

Kenzie avoided meeting his eyes. 'You didn't answer my question about what you and my father talked about while you were out,' she reminded him, determined to stay clear of any conversation that might cause an argument.

He shrugged, slowly sitting up. 'This and that,' he dismissed, his gaze unwavering on her. 'Nothing of importance.'

Unless you counted Donald's satisfaction in knowing that, after tomorrow, all of his girls would be happily married and settled.

It was a sentiment that gave Dominick an insight into the difficulty Kenzie must have felt in breaking the news of their separation to her family—he hadn't felt in a position to disappoint the older man either!

'You never did tell me how Jerome Carlton rates as a lover?' he looked up as he challenged her.

Dominick had realized the last few days that he still couldn't stand the thought of anyone else touching her silken curves, and all those secret, erotic places only he had known. He still hated the idea of someone else hearing her little cries of pleasure as she reached the pinnacle of her sensual enjoyment. And the thought of Kenzie kissing and caressing any other man in the way she had him still had the effect of making his stomach clench into knots!

Kenzie studied Dominick for several seconds, wondering if he actually cared if she'd had another lover, and whether it had been jealousy all along that had caused him to cut her out of his life with so much finality.

But the glittering of his dark eyes and the tightness of his jaw were evidence of cold anger rather than the jealousy she had been hoping for. By bringing Jerome back into the conversation at all he was just spoiling for another fight.

She raised her chin defiantly. 'As it isn't gentlemanly of a man to tell tales out of the bedroom, I'm sure it isn't ladylike for a woman to do so, either—Dominick, what are you doing?' she demanded incredulously as he sprang up off the bed to grasp her by the tops of her arms. 'Let me go!' she instructed impatiently, glaring up at him. 'You don't really care whether or not Jerome and I have been lovers—'

'Don't I?' he grated.

She shook her head, her hair silky about her shoulders. 'You have to feel love to care, Dominick!'

He became suddenly still, maintaining a firm hold of her arms, his face only inches from her own. 'Perhaps I'm just wondering how your parents would feel if they knew their little Kenzie had been sleeping around.'

She glared at him. 'I thought what we were discussing had nothing to do with sleeping!'

'You little—' He broke off abruptly, drawing in deep, controlling breaths as he continued to scowl down at her.

Kenzie was tall and usually found herself on a level with most men, but Dominick had always been four or five inches taller than her, and that impression of height, along with the powerful width of his shoulders, became even more apparent as he strove to regain control of the anger she had deliberately incited.

'But you don't care, Dominick,' she taunted coolly, determined to meet the furious glitter of his eyes. 'You never did. Because you don't believe in love, remember?' she mocked, recalling the painful disillusionment the moment she had realized that.

No, he didn't believe in love, Dominick acknowledged, and he had no idea *what* he felt for Kenzie at that moment, only that the thought of her in Jerome Carlton's arms was once again driving him crazy.

There hadn't been any other women in his life during the four months of their separation. Having Kenzie walk out on him in that way, leaving him for another man, seemed to have killed all desire for sex in him.

Until the second he had seen Kenzie on Wednesday evening...

Since then he had been filled with nothing *but* a desire for sex. But only with Kenzie.

But not here. And not now. That would happen on his terms. For his pleasure.

His hands dropped abruptly to his sides as he released her. 'I don't believe in love,' he said abruptly. 'I'll go and use the bathroom myself now. And I didn't make provision for sharing a bedroom for the night with my ex-wife, so, if you don't want to be shocked out of your romantic little mind, I should turn over and go to sleep before I get back!' He strode over to the adjoining room and pulled the door shut firmly behind him.

Kenzie stared at the closed door, blinking back the tears that threatened to fall. She knew there was no hope for her and Dominick, no common ground of conversation even. There was just anger and misunderstanding on Dominick's part, and love, still love, on hers...

'For God's sake settle down and go to sleep, will you?' Dominick snapped softly in the darkness of the bedroom.

Kenzie became still in the adjoining bed. 'Sorry. I didn't think you were awake,' she muttered, having had no idea he had been aware of her restless movements for the last hour as sleep had eluded her.

He gave a heavy sigh. 'You may think I lack a certain—insight where emotions are concerned, Kenzie, but I can assure you there is absolutely nothing wrong with my memory!'

And what was that supposed to mean?

That he was still thinking about her with Jerome Carlton?

Or something else…?

'I can't sleep,' she sighed.

'I think that's pretty damned obvious!' he bit out tersely. 'Unfortunately, now neither can I!'

'Sorry,' she muttered again.

Dominick sat up in the bed, swinging his legs to the floor as he pushed the duvet aside.

He could see very little of Kenzie in the moonlight shining in through the window, only the paleness of her face and the dark cloud of her hair spread out on the pillow beside her.

'Do you want me to come over there?' he taunted.

No, of course she didn't!

Did she…?

There was no denying that she was totally aware of him, and had been so since he'd called at her apartment earlier this afternoon. Sharing this bedroom with him, even in separate beds, was absolute torture to her senses.

She hadn't thought it would be like this. Yes, she still loved Dominick, and, yes, she was still very aware of his physical attractiveness, but she had thought his total distrust of her, and his lack of love for her, would have killed all the sexual *desire* she had once felt for him.

In the last hour while she had lain here unable to sleep, she had been all too conscious of Dominick in the adjoining bed: of the even tenor of breathing, the slightly elusive tang of his aftershave, and of the heat of his body. All of which had shown her that she ached for him just as much as she ever had.

'No, of course I don't want you to come over here,' she answered without conviction.

'Are you sure?'

She bristled at his mocking tone of voice. 'Of course I'm sure!'

'You didn't sound very sure,' Dominick mused.

'I'm not going to deny that this situation is—difficult,' she told him quietly.

'How difficult?' he challenged, standing up, his lithe nakedness visible in the soft light.

Kenzie stopped breathing, her eyes wide as she looked at him. This was not a good idea. Not a good idea at all.

'Look, Dominick,' she told him quickly. 'I'm sure we could quite easily make love together, here and now—'

'We could?' he derided.

'Yes,' she bit out awkwardly. 'Statistics show that the majority of married couples who have separated have sex together at least once after that separation before they actually divorce. It's usually a disappointment to both parties, and only serves to reaffirm their decision—'

'I'm not interested in statistics, Kenzie,' he dismissed impatiently. 'And you have never disappointed me in bed, any more than I believe I have ever disappointed you, either—'

'You're talking about sex again, Dominick,' she cut in frustratedly.

He gave a shake of his head, moving until he sat on the edge of her bed. 'And talking has never solved anything between us, has it?' he acknowledged ruefully, one of his hands moving up to smooth the creamy contour of her cheek. 'The truth is, I would much rather show you what you threw away four months ago than talk about it!' His head lowered before his lips captured hers.

Kenzie fought against the desire that quickly rose within her, pushing at the bareness of his chest as she wrenched her mouth from his. 'No—'

'Yes, Kenzie!' he insisted gruffly. 'Neither of us is going to find a moment's rest until we get this out of the way!'

'But it won't solve anything—'

'It will prove that you still want me!' he grated. 'Because you do still want me, don't you, Kenzie?' he encouraged huskily as his fingers trailed down her neck to the hollows of her throat.

Kenzie quivered with an awareness she was unable to hide. 'You're just trying to punish me, Dominick. Wreak some sort of revenge because I dared to leave you—'

'Oh, no, Kenzie, a brief time together at the home of your parents isn't going to be nearly enough recompense for that,' he assured her grimly. 'But a little down payment might not be a bad idea in the circumstances. And you do owe me, remember…?'

Oh, she remembered, all right. She also had a pretty good idea now of exactly what he was going to want in 'payment' for being here with her this weekend!

'Dominick—'

'Not now, Kenzie,' he dismissed, his hand moving down to cup her breast, his thumbtip caressing the hardened tip as he bent his head to reclaim her lips.

Kenzie felt the heat in her body, wanting to continue

fighting him, but knowing that her body betrayed her. She melted through her enjoyment of the feel of Dominick's lips on hers as he began to kiss her, and found she was unable to stop herself from reaching up to entangle her fingers in his hair as she tasted him in return.

His hands moved restlessly across her back, moulding her body to his, and crushing her breasts against the hardness of his chest as they continued to kiss hungrily.

Kenzie groaned low in her throat as Dominick sat back slightly to push the gaping neckline of her top to one side, one hand finding her naked breast, while the other moved to unfasten the buttons down the front of the silky garment.

She felt the cool air on her bare flesh as Dominick cleared the material from her body, his lips leaving hers now so that he could feel the thrust of her breast with his mouth. As he drew the aching nipple into the heated moisture between his lips, the pad of his thumb moving across its twin, Kenzie dropped weakly back onto the pillow as she arched in pleasure.

She could feel his arousal pressed against her, an ache between her own thighs matching that need.

Her fingers tightened in his hair as she pulled him even closer, feeling the rasp of his tongue now, circling and flicking the tip of her breast, before drawing it into his mouth to suck rhythmically.

The heat was rapidly building inside her as she reached out to touch him, her fingers closing about him, revelling in the wild pulsing. She moved her hand along the length of the hardened shaft, knowing, as she always had, how to pleasure him.

He lifted his head, his eyes glittering in the darkness. 'Do you want me to take you, Kenzie?' he asked. 'Do you want me inside you?'

'Yes! Oh, God, yes!' she groaned, completely, mindlessly, aroused.

'How much do you want me, Kenzie?' His hand lightly touched her breast. 'Tell me how much!'

'Dominick…?' She looked up at him, feeling dazed.

'How much, Kenzie?' His voice hardened slightly.

'Dominick, what do you want from me?' she moaned, the desire he had aroused completely confusing her.

'Right now?' he considered as he sat up to move away from her. 'Nothing else for now,' he murmured with satisfaction. 'When I next take you to bed, Kenzie—and I am going to take you to bed—it's going to be on my terms, and when I choose. Tonight was just to see if you're as immune to me as you claimed to be when you walked out on me.' His teeth gleamed in the moonlight as he smiled. 'You aren't immune at all, Kenzie,' he taunted.

No, she wasn't. But this wasn't the way. This would never be the way…

'Please don't do this, Dominick,' she warned breathlessly. 'Don't destroy what feelings of respect we have left for each other—'

'*Me* destroy those feelings?' He surged to his feet to stand darkly forbidding beside the bed as he looked down at her with hard, glittering eyes. '*You* did that when you walked out the door four months ago!'

Yes, she had walked out—and, although Dominick might not believe it, it had almost killed her to do it.

Did Dominick really imagine that it had been easy for her to leave, to give up on the hope that he would one day love her as she loved him? Because if he really thought that—

'Straight into Jerome Carlton's arms and bed!' he added harshly.

Jerome Carlton again.

It always came back to Jerome.

Kenzie had no idea why Dominick was so convinced she'd had an affair with the other man.

All that Jerome had done was offer her a contract with his company, and had been there for her when she'd sat beside him on the plane to America, still slightly shell-shocked from the last argument with Dominick. Jerome had obviously not known exactly why she was so unhappy, but he had been there for her anyway, and he had continued to be attentive during the weeks she'd spent in America when she had seemed so unhappy.

He had asked nothing in return.

But Dominick wouldn't understand that. He didn't understand that there could be just friendship between a man and a woman. He didn't understand love between a man and a woman, so how could he possibly understand friendship?

'Please, don't do anything that is going to make me hate you, Dominick,' she pleaded forcefully, not sure she would be able to bear that when she loved him so much.

He gave a humourless laugh. 'Why not? They say that hate is akin to love! Either emotion has to be an improvement on that coolness you showed me for the month before you ended the torture of our marriage. It has to be better than the distant politeness with which you've been treating me all evening!'

But that distant politeness was her protection, Kenzie

thought. It was the only thing she had to stop this man from making her suffer more than he was already.

She couldn't let Dominick hurt her all over again; she had barely survived the first time!

'Get some sleep, Kenzie,' he advised harshly as he began to pull on his clothes.

'Where are you going?' She frowned.

'I have no idea,' he grated after pulling his tee shirt on over his head. 'But don't worry, Kenzie, I'm not leaving.' He paused to look down at her. 'I don't like weddings, but I've said I'll fulfil my half of the bargain, and so I will. Just be prepared, when the time comes, to fulfil yours!'

CHAPTER SIX

KENZIE had no idea where Dominick had spent the night, only knowing that he hadn't come back to the bedroom they should have shared.

She knew he hadn't returned because she had spent most of the night awake, too troubled, and too disturbed by what had happened, to be able to fall asleep.

A fact that the bathroom mirror had all too readily confirmed when she went through to shower and dress this morning, dark circles under her eyes, and her face pale.

A great glowing bridesmaid she was going to make, she thought as she put on enough make-up to cover up her pallor.

Just the thought of facing Dominick again, after the intimacies they had shared during the night, wasn't something she relished.

Although she knew it was something she wasn't going to have a choice about. Dominick had said he wouldn't leave, and she knew him well enough by now to know that when he said something he meant it. He intended staying for the wedding.

If only so that he could collect on his half of their bargain.

Exactly what sort of revenge did Dominick intend exacting?

Although after what he had said last night, and the way he had so deliberately kissed and caressed her, she didn't really need to ask that!

But could he really want to take her like that, to make love to her and know that she hated every minute of it?

Except she so obviously wouldn't…!

After her response last night Dominick couldn't be in any doubts about that, either.

His revenge, she was sure, would be to make love to her and show her exactly how little will-power she really had where he was concerned. He wanted to prove that she still wanted him, in spite of herself.

When and where he intended this to take place, she had no idea, but she knew that it wasn't going to be here.

It was like waiting for the other shoe to drop, although it was a little hard to place the vengeful Dominick she'd seen last night in the man she discovered in the kitchen a few minutes later. He was with her mother, trying on the bow-tie that matched the deep green colour of the bridesmaid dresses that he was expected to wear as her partner at the wedding.

It was a little unnerving to hear Dominick's throaty laughter and her mother's girlish chuckles when Kenzie had been steeling herself to face her arrogant and demanding husband of last night.

Admittedly Dominick did look slightly ridiculous with the bow-tie around his neck above the black tee shirt, but Kenzie didn't think it was funny enough for this amount of hilarity…

She stood in the kitchen doorway simply staring at the two of them, marvelling at this slightly softer Dominick, and wondering if he was actually aware of how relaxed he looked. Probably not.

Dominick didn't let his guard down often. And last night he had made it pretty plain that with her he didn't intend letting his barriers down at all.

Nevertheless, it was still a little unnerving to see Dominick so relaxed and at ease with her mother. Unless it was all an act? Was this all an effort on his part to show he was keeping to his side of their bargain?

That was probably nearer the truth!

'Am I interrupting something?' Kenzie finally murmured.

Dominick's laughter faded quickly, his expression mockingly questioning as he turned to look at her.

Confirming to Kenzie that he really was just continuing the act, and that he intended giving her no reason whatsoever to complain about his behaviour in front of her family.

Her mother continued to smile. 'Dominick and I were just thinking he looks like one of those male strippers—just before he whips his clothes off and leaves on only the bow-tie.'

Kenzie deliberately didn't look at Dominick again as her dark brows raised towards her mother. 'And when did you last see a male stripper?'

The last time Kenzie had seen Dominick, he had actually been naked so there was no way she could meet his gaze at the moment!

'Never.' Her mother gave an exaggerated sigh of disappointment.

'Mother!' Kenzie chuckled affectionately.

Nancy shook her head ruefully as she gave a smile that encompassed Dominick as well as Kenzie. 'That's the trouble with you youngsters—you think you were the first to discover the attractions of the naked body!'

'Not me,' Dominick drawled, having discovered this morning that, in spite of his usual reticence, he actually liked this older version of Kenzie. He was finding it very hard to remain aloof from the happiness this family felt on the day of the youngest daughter's wedding. 'It's obvious that you and Donald discovered it at least four times in the last thirty years!' he teased.

Nancy gave a becoming blush. 'I guess I deserved that one!' She grinned. 'Kenzie, I have to go and telephone the florist and find out why the flowers haven't arrived yet, so I'll leave you to get Dominick some breakfast.' She gave her daughter an affectionate pat on the cheek as she moved to the door. 'Don't forget we're leaving for the hairdresser's in half an hour,' she reminded her before going to make her call.

Now Dominick and Kenzie were alone in the kitchen, although it was obvious from the closing of doors overhead, and the sound of loud voices, that they were far from the only people in the house.

Dominick reached up and unfastened the bow-tie from around his neck to hold it loosely between his fingers as he looked across at Kenzie.

She looked about sixteen this morning, dressed in

those jeans and a fitted green tee shirt the colour of her eyes, the silky length of her hair secured in a band.

She raised her long dark lashes and met his gaze, memories of their time together last night deep in their depths.

They were the same memories that had haunted Dominick for the rest of the night as he'd sat down here in the kitchen drinking coffee. Half of him had wanted to go back upstairs and finish what they had started, but the other half of him had known this wasn't the time or the place. What happened between him and Kenzie in the future had to be on his terms. Anything else was unacceptable.

Kenzie had walked out on him, and he didn't intend letting her get away from him again until he had exacted his pound of flesh in payment for that.

Literally!

In the meantime he was determined to keep strictly to his side of the bargain, giving Kenzie no way out of fulfilling her side. None at all. However unacceptable to her his terms turned out to be…

'Your mother mentioned something about breakfast,' he reminded her abruptly, more for something to say than any real appetite. Although he had so much coffee in his system it probably wouldn't be a bad idea to eat something.

Kenzie drew in a ragged breath. Whatever she had been expecting Dominick to say it certainly hadn't been something as prosaic as requesting breakfast.

Although the alternative, discussing what had happened last night, wasn't a good idea, either!

'Of course.' She moved to search through one of the

cupboards. 'I'm afraid we're more geared to the wedding today than—ah, toast or cereal, or both?'

'Cereal will be fine,' he assured her dismissively. 'What are you having done to your hair?' he questioned as he got the milk from the fridge and carried it over to the table.

'It's going to be styled into curls with peach-coloured flowers entwined,' she answered, her thoughts elsewhere as she carried over a couple of boxes of cereal and two bowls to the table, placing them down before sitting opposite him. 'Dominick—'

'I had no idea there was so much planning and organization involved in a wedding,' he cut in determinedly, knowing by the frown on her face that he wasn't going to like what she'd been about to say. 'Ah,' he murmured, looking at the two cereal boxes, 'Flakes or flakes!'

She grimaced. 'Everyone is a little—distracted, today.'

'Understandable in the circumstances.' He nodded, pouring the milk over his cereal.

They couldn't even talk to each other any more, Kenzie realized with a pained wince as she poured herself a cup of black coffee, acutely aware that Dominick hadn't found the same awkwardness when talking to her mother earlier, or having fun over a bow-tie.

'You missed out on all of this, didn't you?' he suddenly remarked thoughtfully.

Kenzie blinked, looking up at him with a frown. 'Living at home? But I moved to London years ago—'

'I'm not talking about the living at home, Kenzie,' he said impatiently, putting his spoon down in the barely touched cereal and pushing the bowl away, the darkness of his gaze easily holding her. 'Wouldn't you have liked your wedding to be like this? The excitement of a church wedding, with all your family around you, instead of being whisked off to Las Vegas in the way that you were?'

'Well…yes, it would have been nice,' she acknowledged slowly. 'But it wasn't what you wanted—'

'I don't believe I was talking about what I wanted,' Dominick stated, sitting back in his chair to look at her analytically.

Kenzie avoided meeting his piercing gaze. 'I don't think talking about this now serves any purpose whatsoever, Dominick,' she told him wearily, pushing away her empty coffee-cup.

'Why's that?' he challenged. 'Has Carlton already promised you the white dress when the two of you get married?'

Kenzie drew in a sharp breath at the deliberate provocation. 'Even if he felt that way about me—which he doesn't!—I have no intentions of marrying Jerome Carlton. Or indeed any other man. Believe me, Dominick—' she stood up '—once our divorce is final I will be a lot more cautious before I even *think* about getting married again!'

Dominick reached out to grasp her arm. 'The feeling is mutual, I do assure you!' he grated harshly.

'We only have another twelve hours or so to get through together today, Dominick, can't we at least try to be civilized about this?' she reasoned, grimacing.

'I think I'm being extremely civilized,' he bit out evenly.

He probably was for him, she thought heavily. Dominick was a man who took what he wanted when he couldn't get it any other way, and having her walk out on him, on their marriage—and, as far as he was concerned, into the arms of another man—must have dented that Masters pride more than a little.

More than a little? Having her walk out on him in that way had probably infuriated him!

What a fool she had been to put herself back in his power like this. Worse, she had now given Dominick the ideal opportunity he needed to exact his revenge. Not even the happiness she had seen on her father's face last night was enough to take away the trepidation she felt about that!

She twisted her arm in an effort to release it from his grasp, but only succeeded in tightening his grip. 'You're hurting me, Dominick,' she told him quietly.

His smile was humourless. 'You don't know the meaning of the word!' he rasped as he released her abruptly.

'More than you do, I'm certain!' Kenzie replied angrily, resisting the temptation she had to rub the reddened skin of her wrist. 'I'm sure my parents will understand if you want to make your excuses and return to London tonight instead of in the morning,' she told him briskly. 'I can easily get a train back tomorrow. And this way you can get back to your own life all the sooner.'

She really wanted him out of here, didn't she? Dominick realized in frustration.

Out of her family home.

Out of her family's life.

Out of *her* life.

And for the last four months he had thought that was the best thing for them too, that he should never have married Kenzie in the first place, and that her leaving him only served to confirm the cynicism he had always felt for the institution.

Nevertheless, standing impotently by as Kenzie walked out of his life had been the hardest thing he had ever done. Not that there had ever been the least possibility that he would ask her to stay, but after nine months of being married to her, suddenly finding himself once again living alone, eating alone, and sleeping alone, had been much harder than he had thought it was going to be.

For weeks he had raged about the place, critical of everything and everyone, so angry with Kenzie, with Jerome Carlton, but mainly with himself, because he'd known that in spite of everything he still wanted her.

But, he had told himself, he had lived alone before Kenzie came into his life, and he would survive on his own now that she had chosen to go.

And he *had* survived. If continuing to wake, work, eat and sleep could be called surviving...

But now Kenzie was back. Not to stay, but back nonetheless, and he had every intention of slaking his thirst for her delectable body once and for all!

His mouth twisted humorously. 'I'm not going anywhere, Kenzie. We leave here together tomorrow as planned.'

She drew in a ragged breath, having been afraid that would be his answer. 'If you'll excuse me? I have to go and get ready to go to the hairdresser's.' She didn't so much as glance at him again before leaving the room, hating what they were doing to each other, but unable to find a way to stop it.

If what she suspected was going to be Dominick's revenge, then this destruction was only going to get worse...

CHAPTER SEVEN

KENZIE was as tense as a young colt as she sat beside him at the wedding reception, Dominick noted with a scowl. The meal was over, the speeches just coming to a close, and Kenzie had been tense through all of it.

What had she thought he was going to do, for goodness' sake, stand up in the church in the middle of the marriage ceremony and pronounce that marriage, and their own marriage, was nothing but a sham?

That would make rather a nonsense of the last torturous twenty-four hours, and Kenzie should know him well enough by now to know that he abhorred wasting his time, on anything.

He had been more than prepared to play his part today, and had been gracious and charming to the rest of Kenzie's family as Nancy had introduced him.

What he hadn't been prepared for was the sight of Kenzie walking down the aisle behind Kathy. The floating green dress she wore, and the flowers entwined in the darkness of her hair, made her somehow look like a fairy princess.

It had given him something of a jolt, he had to admit,

but it had been a weakness he had quickly brought back under control. Kenzie was playing a part just as much as he was, and the truth was she was no more a fairy princess than he was Prince Charming!

'Oh, look!' Kenzie murmured happily now as her cheeks became flushed, and her eyes glowed. 'Kathy and Derek are going to start the dancing!'

Dancing?

Of course there would be dancing, Dominick told himself impatiently. Weddings weren't his favourite things, but he'd had no choice but to attend one or two of them in the past—including too many of his own parents'—and there was always dancing after the speeches.

Had he ever danced with Kenzie?

No, he couldn't say that he had…

'Shall we join them?'

Kenzie turned from gazing indulgently at her youngest sister and her new husband, who had eyes for no one but each other as they slowly danced, to look up at Dominick as he stood beside her chair. His expression and eyes were unreadable as he held his hand out to her in invitation.

'I think it's expected,' he growled as she made no effort to get to her feet, and he glanced pointedly at the two sets of parents and her sisters and their husbands dancing.

Of course it was expected, Kenzie acknowledged heavily. She was a bridesmaid. Dominick was her husband.

'People are starting to stare, Kenzie,' he whispered as she continued to look at him without speaking.

'Of course,' she accepted gracefully, taking his hand as she stood up, knowing that would be expected of her too.

His hand was firm and dry to the touch, and his fingers curled lightly about hers as he led her onto the dance floor. Her breath caught in her throat as he turned to take her into his arms, keeping his hand in hers as his other arm moved lightly about her waist to draw her close against him.

Kenzie could feel her pulse racing as they began to move to the music, she was so physically aware of Dominick: the warmth of his body enveloping her, the softness of his breath gently stirring the loose tendrils of hair at her temples.

He danced gracefully, easily guiding her movements to match his own. Not that she had ever expected anything else. Dominick did everything well. More than well. Business deals. Dancing. Making love…

She stumbled slightly at that last thought. Despite the busyness of the day, the memories of their lovemaking the previous night had never been far from her mind, and being held close to Dominick like this was only increasing her desire for him.

'Steady,' Dominick warned as his arms tightened more securely about her. He concentrated totally on her, seeming unconcerned that the other wedding guests were watching the couples circling the dance floor.

Dominick could think of nothing else but holding Kenzie in his arms as they danced. She was almost as tall as him in her heeled green satin shoes, and she was like gossamer in his arms, seeming to float around the floor. The image of a fairy princess became even more acute and yet he could still feel her tension.

'For goodness' sake relax, Kenzie,' he muttered impatiently. 'One thing you can be sure of, I'm not about to ravish you in the middle of a dance floor!'

Her eyes were like huge green lakes in the paleness of her face as she looked up at him. 'I never for a moment thought that you were,' she told him waspishly, her chin raised in challenge.

'Didn't you?' he mocked.

'No!' Her eyes flashed. 'I—the dance has ended,' she realized with obvious relief, stepping away from him to turn and applaud the bride and groom, her face once more glowing as she watched her younger sister's obvious happiness.

Dominick's gaze remained fixed on Kenzie, taking in the arch of her brows, the eyes glowing beneath long dark lashes, the curve of her cheek, those full, passionate lips, and the smooth line of her jaw.

Beautiful.

Kenzie was still the most beautiful woman he had ever seen.

His wife.

But not his wife.

Maybe not, but she wasn't any other man's wife yet. And she still owed him…

'Thank you once again for all that you did this weekend,' Kenzie told Dominick late Sunday morning as she got out of the car he had parked outside her apartment building.

She felt a surge of relief that it was all over, and she could finally get away from Dominick's domineering presence.

Not that he hadn't continued to behave impeccably during the rest of their stay at her parents' house. It was just the fact that he was there that was so unnerving.

And she hadn't slept well again last night. Dominick hadn't seemed to have the same trouble, the even tenor of his breathing telling her that he had fallen asleep almost as soon as his head had touched the pillow.

She had thought only the innocent slept like that—and innocent was something Dominick most certainly wasn't!

He was out of the car now and standing on the pavement beside her, her overnight bag in his hand. 'I'll take this up for you,' he offered lightly.

'There's no need,' she refused, frowning. 'I can easily carry it myself.'

'I'm sure you can.' He nodded, his smile derisive. 'But you must realize we haven't finished discussing this—transaction, yet,' he reminded her softly.

Kenzie's shoulders stiffened, her chin lifting as she met his challenging gaze. 'I'm not in the mood right now, Dominick!'

'The mood for what?'

Her cheeks flushed with anger. 'For whatever you have in mind!'

Dominick smiled, his eyes darkening, and his teeth very white against the tanned skin. 'Right now I have it in mind to take your bag upstairs for you and let you make me a cup of coffee. If I change my mind about any of that, I'll let you know!'

Despite his mockery Kenzie was still reluctant to invite Dominick up to her apartment. Not because she had anything to hide. She simply didn't want his presence there, in the private space she had made for herself the last few months. Dominick had nothing to do with her life as it was now, and after being with him again this weekend that was the way she wanted it to stay.

'Kenzie, didn't last night prove to you that I'm not filled with unrestrained lust every time I'm alone with you?' he taunted scathingly at her continued silence.

Her blush deepened. 'I never thought that you were!'

'Didn't you?' he questioned, a glint in his eye.

'No,' she assured stubbornly. 'Look, Dominick, you've had your fun with me—'

'My dear Kenzie, I haven't even *begun* to have fun yet!' he promised.

His idea of fun and hers were vastly different, then!

'Besides,' he added softly, 'we really do need to discuss what you're going to give me in return for this weekend.'

'Give you?' she echoed sharply.

'Give me,' Dominick repeated softly, reaching up to smooth the frown from between her eyes. 'Don't frown, Kenzie, you'll get lines. And then what would Carlton Cosmetics, and especially Jerome Carlton, have to say?' His mouth had tightened perceptibly.

At that moment, she didn't give a damn what Carlton Cosmetics—or Jerome!—had to say about anything. She was far more concerned with what Dominick would want from her, what he would demand she give, after he had so generously given up this weekend for her.

It didn't help that the skin on her forehead tingled where he had touched her!

'Fine,' she snapped, taking her bag from him. 'Then you had better come up and discuss it, hadn't you?'

Dominick watched with narrowed eyes as she turned and walked away, enjoying the sensual sway of her slender hips in her tight jeans and the way her hair cascaded down the length of her spine.

She was his.

Every sensual, delectable inch of her was going to be his again. She just didn't know it yet.

He was smiling when he stepped into the lift she had held for him, that smile widening as he could sense her deepening annoyance as the lift ascended. An angry, spitting Kenzie was much easier to deal with than that coolly dismissive one!

'Come in,' she invited tersely after unlocking the door to her apartment and going inside to throw her overnight bag down on a chair.

Dominick took his time, looking around him with interest. The apartment was decorated with soft autumn colours interspersed with touches of emerald-green and Mediterranean-blue, and the prints on the walls were of dreamy scenes from the late nineteenth century, with women in floaty dresses and hats, and men wearing frock coats.

In sharp contrast, his own apartment, where he had taken Kenzie after they were married, was very contemporary, with lots of glass and chrome and leather furnishings, the paintings on the walls originals by up-and-coming modern day artists.

He had never realized Kenzie's tastes were so different from his.

Having spent the weekend with Kenzie's family in the ex-vicarage set within its acre of garden, Dominick recognized that the village girl in Kenzie was still very much alive.

'Nice.' He nodded appreciatively as he turned back to look at Kenzie.

A very tense Kenzie, he thought, who looked as if she

expected, despite what he had said downstairs, him to pounce on her at any moment.

Well, she was going to be disappointed.

He'd really meant it when he'd told her he had no intention of collecting on his side of their bargain now. No, he intended to prolong that satisfaction for as long as possible. He'd wanted to make her suffer a little, in the same way he suffered every time he imagined her in Jerome Carlton's bed!

Kenzie gave an impatient shake of her head, not interested in what he did or didn't think of her apartment. 'Just say what you have to say and then go.' She glared, not at all comfortable with his invasion into her private sanctuary.

Instead of doing any such thing Dominick dropped down into one of her big overstuffed terracotta-coloured armchairs. 'You aren't being very polite, Kenzie,' he drawled. 'I told you I could do with a coffee after the drive.'

'It's usual to ask!' she snapped irritably.

His dark brows raised mockingly over his amused brown eyes. 'A black coffee would be much appreciated, thank you.'

'Have a hangover, do you?' she came back tartly, thinking she really would end up with lines if she didn't stop frowning so much!

'Sorry to disappoint you, but not at all. I only had one glass of champagne at the wedding reception, and from experience it isn't a drink that gives me a hangover,' he replied, completely unconcerned by her bad humour. 'As I'm sure you remember, I happen to prefer my coffee black.'

Getting him the coffee wasn't the problem, especially as it meant she could escape into the kitchen for a few minutes' respite from his disturbing company. It was the time he was going to spend in her apartment drinking it that was the problem.

He hadn't told her what he wanted from her yet, and she very much doubted he would leave until he had.

She didn't doubt that Dominick was enjoying himself, his air of amusement having become much more pronounced this morning.

Away from her close-knit family, Kenzie was having more trouble, and much less opportunity, to remain aloof from him. Which, of course, was exactly what he wanted.

Damn him.

Dominick relaxed back in his chair as Kenzie left the room, easing the tiredness from his body. Last night, he had pretended to be sleeping, he had lain awake long after Kenzie had finally fallen asleep.

Plotting.

Planning.

Savouring.

He was not going to rush something that was giving him so much pleasure just thinking about it.

'Here,' she said briskly. when she returned from the kitchen and handed him the cup of black coffee.

'Thank you,' he said with exaggerated politeness. 'Aren't you joining me?' he prompted lightly as she dropped down into the chair opposite to look across at him broodingly.

'Just tell me what you want from me, Dominick,' she snapped. 'And let's stop playing games!'

'You really aren't being very—gracious, are you, now that I've kept my side of the bargain?' he chided.

Kenzie opened her mouth to give him another sharp reply, instead firmly closing it again, her lips clamping together as she realized that he was only speaking the truth.

But he was the one who had made a bargain of this and only after she had told him she really would be very grateful if he would do her this favour…

Yes, but—

No buts. She had said that, and that was exactly what he had done. Was it any wonder that he now wanted payment?

'Sorry,' she muttered between stiff lips. 'What is it you want from me, Dominick?'

'Well, let's get one thing straight from the first, shall we?' He put his coffee cup down to sit forward in his chair, his expression intent, his gaze narrowed as he looked deep into her eyes. 'I have never been into taking unwilling women into my bed!'

He had never needed to, she thought. Before the two of them had met Dominick had been known for his numerous affairs with glamorous, beautiful women, affairs that he had always ended rather than the other way around. In fact, she was probably the first woman to ever walk away from him!

Which was the reason for Dominick's anger, of course…

But they couldn't just—she couldn't just—

Going to bed with Dominick in that way, so cold and calculated, was completely against the way she had lived her life so far. But all of Dominick's comments so far over the course of the weekend seemed to suggest that was exactly what he was going to demand.

Kenzie willed herself to calm down, to settle into the mental relaxation she often escaped to during the long, interminable waits she experienced between photographic shoots. She tried to breathe deeply and evenly, and was able to meet Dominick's gaze quite calmly when she looked at him.

After all, hadn't he just told her that he wouldn't take an unwilling woman to his bed?

She would just have to try to ensure, no matter what the provocation, that she was never willing!

Dominick stood up abruptly, moving over to look at the bookcase along one wall of the room. 'You obviously like to read.' He nodded at the well-thumbed rows of paperbacks lined on the shelves.

'Yes,' she acknowledged quietly, slightly thrown by his change of subject.

He nodded. 'So do I. In fact, I've read most of these titles, too.'

Her eyes widened in spite of herself. 'I never remember you reading anything but contracts and the business section of the newspaper when we were together!'

He shrugged broad shoulders. 'That's probably because we always found plenty of other things to do when we were together other than reading fiction books.'

Like making love.

How strange that she should learn now, after living apart for months, that the two of them actually had a similar taste in reading.

What else was there about him, other small personal details, that she hadn't had the opportunity to learn during their nine months of marriage? All they had been able to think about at the time, all that had interested either of them when they hadn't been caught up in their individual business commitments, was being with each other...

Dominick could see the surprise, and the puzzled interest, in Kenzie's eyes, and decided that he had probably gone far enough for one day. The best way to succeed in anything, he had learnt over the years, was to always walk away leaving the other person wanting more, wondering...

And he did intend succeeding where Kenzie was concerned. In not only getting her back into his bed, but getting her there willingly. Willingly was the most important part, if she did but know it!

He bent to put his empty cup on the low coffee-table before straightening. 'Are you free next weekend?'

'I—yes, I think so,' Kenzie confirmed vaguely, obviously surprised by the question as she stood up to follow him to the door.

Dominick paused in the open doorway. 'Then keep it free, hmm?'

'Why?' she said sharply.

He shook his head. 'I have—some details, to finalize, before I can confirm that. Perhaps we could have dinner together one night in the week—'

'Dinner?' she repeated in frustration, shaking her head. 'Dominick, I'm not going out on a date with you!'

'—so that we can discuss this further,' he finished pointedly, his brows rising over reproving brown eyes.

'But—'

'In the same way that we met for dinner last week

when you wanted to discuss your sister's wedding with me, remember?' he reminded, in a mocking tone.

'Oh. Yes.' She looked uncomfortable now.

'Although I would like the two of us to actually eat something this time!' he added derisively.

'Don't take me to Rimini's, then,' Kenzie told him firmly. 'It would remind me too much of when we used to go there together when we were married,' she added dismissively as he gave her a questioning look.

When they were married?

They were still married, damn it!

But if it meant Kenzie would relax a little, he was quite happy to fall in with her suggestion that they go somewhere else. Somewhere new, perhaps, where the restaurant didn't remind either of them of someone else.

His mouth thinned as he thought of Kenzie's 'someone else'.

'Or when you went there with Jerome, perhaps?' he asked impatiently.

Kenzie gave an irritated shake of her head. 'You know, Dominick—' she sighed in despair '—one day you're going to actually listen to me when I tell you I wasn't involved with Jerome Carlton four months ago, and that I'm not involved with him now, either!'

'Oh, I listen, Kenzie,' Dominick assured her. 'I just happen to know that you aren't telling the truth!'

She could accept that the fact she had spent so much time in Jerome Carlton's company just before she'd left Dominick, and that when she had left it had been to fly to America with the other man, could have all looked more than a little suspicious to Dominick's accusing eyes.

But what she hadn't accepted then, and still didn't

accept, was that Dominick hadn't even attempted to believe her denials. He had seemed convinced from the outset that she was involved in an affair with Jerome, and nothing she said or did would convince him otherwise.

She certainly wasn't convincing him now, she thought, seeing the cold scepticism in the hardness of his eyes.

'Let me know about dinner, hmm?' she prompted abruptly, really wanting—needing!—him to leave now, the strain she had been under this weekend definitely starting to catch up with her.

'Oh, I'll let you know, Kenzie,' he assured her, seeing that strain in her eyes, and the paleness of her cheeks, his mouth twisting derisively as he knew just his presence was causing her this distress.

He'd barely begun!

CHAPTER EIGHT

'OKAY, Dominick, that's it! I refuse to let you play this game with me any longer!'

Dominick swivelled his chair slowly from his quiet contemplation of the river flowing smoothly beneath his office window, his eyes fixed in cool enquiry as he looked across the width of his huge oak desk at Kenzie's flushed and angry face.

His gaze moved slightly sideways as he took in his secretary's questioning presence in the open doorway. 'Thanks, Stella,' he said, nodding dismissively.

'Play nice, you two,' she murmured ruefully before backing out of the room and closing the door behind her.

Dominick's gaze returned to Kenzie's annoyed pink face. 'You were saying…?'

Kenzie glared at him, wanting nothing more at that moment than to wipe that smile of self-satisfaction from his handsomely smug face. 'I said I've had enough—'

'I think I understood that bit,' Dominick interrupted, relaxing back in his leather chair. He was dressed formally in a dark business suit, snowy white shirt and silver-coloured tie. 'I'm simply at a loss to know what it is you've had enough of…?'

'I've had enough of you playing with me,' Kenzie bit out fiercely, thinking how arrogant her husband was.

'I think I got that bit too—'

'How dare you have Stella call me up and tell me to meet you at some restaurant called Tonio's at eight o'clock this evening?' she cut in impatiently, knowing that Dominick was enjoying her anger. Damn him!

'Ah.' Dominick nodded in consideration. 'Is eight o'clock too early for you? Or too late, perhaps?'

Kenzie's gaze narrowed dangerously. 'It's this evening that's the problem,' she snapped. 'I haven't just been sitting around all week waiting for you to snap your fingers so I can come running when you do!'

'No?' he questioned mildly. 'Then what have you been doing?'

'I work too, you know,' Kenzie told him impatiently. 'And for your information, I'm busy this evening!' she added with satisfaction.

Even if she hadn't been busy she would have told him she was after his high-handed behaviour.

Dominick eyed her silently for several long seconds, liking this outraged Kenzie much better than the controlled one of the weekend.

Not that her obvious anger made the slightest bit of difference to the outcome of this encounter; annoyed and incensed Kenzie only added to the challenge.

'Why didn't you just tell Stella that when she called?' he prompted mildly. 'Tomorrow evening will do just as well for what I have in mind.'

Although their present location wasn't at all suitable for what he wanted, Dominick acknowledged self-derisively. Kenzie looked so fiercely beautiful, with her hair loose about her shoulders, her eyes blazing green, and that becoming flush to her cheeks. The fitted blouse and pencil-slim black trousers she wore clearly outlined the perfection of her body, and he wanted nothing more than to lay her naked on his desk and make love to her here and now until she cried out for mercy!

But that would not be according to his plan at all, he acknowledged ruefully.

Some of the anger seemed to drain out of Kenzie as her shoulders relaxed slightly. 'And what do you have in mind?' she asked, still eyeing him suspiciously.

He smiled as he gave a mocking shake of his head. 'Dinner and a chat, actually,' he said nonchalantly. 'Unless you can think of anything else we can do to fill the evening?'

The anger snapped back into her deep emerald eyes. 'I told you I refuse to be played with any longer, Dominick,' she said impatiently. 'And now that I'm here, obviously available for that chat, I can't see any reason why we need to have dinner together at all!'

A valid point, he acknowledged—except that it meant Kenzie was taking control of this situation, and that was something he didn't intend letting her do!

Having once allowed circumstances with Kenzie to get out of control enough to find himself marrying her, he had no intention of losing the power a second time.

'My plans still aren't finalized yet, Kenzie,' he told her abruptly. 'But I'm hoping they will be by this evening.'

Kenzie had been doing nothing all week but trying to think what his 'plans' could possibly be—except to know by his comments that those plans seemed to imply he intended taking her to bed at some time in the near future!

Just thinking about that the last three days had been enough to fray her already jangling nerves, until Stella's telephone call earlier today had jettisoned her into doing something about it.

Coming to Dominick's office and confronting him with the situation had seemed to be the answer.

Except it was getting her precisely nowhere. As it was designed not to do, she was sure.

'Have you kept the weekend free as I asked you to do?' he asked.

'Ordered me to do,' she corrected firmly. 'But I don't intend going anywhere with you until I know where and why.'

Dominick put his elbows on his desk, and rested his chin on his laced fingers as he contemplated her through narrowed lids. It was a gaze she easily withstood, her chin raised defiantly. 'You don't seem quite so willing to keep your side of the bargain now that your sister's wedding is over,' he finally murmured dryly.

Kenzie gave a shrug, her head tilted challengingly. 'Maybe I'm not.'

His mouth hardened. 'And maybe I'll just go down and visit your parents tomorrow and explain to them what a sham the two of us being together last weekend actually was!'

Kenzie searched his face, seeing only cold implacability in his hard gaze, his mouth a thin, uncompromising line.

'You would do that too, wouldn't you?' she accepted heavily as she dropped down onto the chair that faced his desk, the anger draining out of her.

She had thought about all of this long and hard since

he'd left her apartment three days ago, and had decided that there was no way Dominick could force her into anything, least of all going to bed with him. Even if he had already made it clear that force wasn't what he had in mind at all where that was concerned!

Somewhere in all her thinking she had forgotten how ruthlessly determined Dominick could be when he felt the situation warranted it. Like now…

'You know that I would,' Dominick confirmed as he saw that knowledge in the pallor of her cheeks. 'Why are you really here, Kenzie?' he prompted with interest, becoming more and more convinced that there was more to her anger than pique over Stella's telephone call.

Kenzie gave him a startled look, like a fawn caught in the headlights of a car. 'I already told you—'

'I heard you,' Dominick cut in dismissively, getting up to come round the desk to stand next to her chair, reaching out to place his hand beneath her chin and lift her face up to his. 'Why, Kenzie?' he repeated harshly, sure that he already knew the answer to that question, but determined to hear her say it nonetheless.

Kenzie tried to move away from the hand beneath her chin, but failed as Dominick's fingers tightened in determination. 'I told you, I don't like being played with—'

'You also told me that you're busy this evening,' he rasped. 'Could I take a guess as to who you're going to be busy with?' he added.

She frowned at him, wondering how he had known, how he could have guessed—

'How could you possibly know Jerome is coming to England?' she said slowly.

Because she was sure that he did know; she could see it in his coldly glittering eyes…

It had been far from ideal timing when Jerome had telephoned her yesterday to inform her he would be arriving in England later today. He wanted to see her this evening to discuss when she would be returning to the States to fulfil her contract for Carlton Cosmetics.

Not having heard from Dominick at the time, and knowing that as he was her current employer she would obviously have to see Jerome some time while he was in England, she had reluctantly agreed. At the same time she had known that it was not a good idea for her to see Jerome at all when Dominick was back in her life, however briefly.

Knowing what Dominick believed her relationship with Jerome to be, the last thing she needed was for the two men to accidentally meet at her apartment of all places!

Stella's phone call earlier this morning, when Kenzie had already agreed to meet Jerome this evening, couldn't have come at a worse time!

Dominick's lips pinched together. 'Just a lucky guess,' he growled, releasing her chin to move back behind his desk. 'Do you still deny that the two of you are involved?'

'Yes, of course I deny it!' Kenzie snapped impatiently. 'Jerome is coming to England on business, and dinner with me this evening is just incidental.'

Dominick looked at her from behind his hooded eyelids, wondering how anyone so beautiful, so innocently beautiful, could at the same time be so deceitful.

'Really?' he questioned scathingly.

'Yes—really!' she echoed irritably. 'Not that I expect

you to believe me.' She shook her head. 'You seem to take some sort of delight in not believing me!'

'I don't take delight in it at all, Kenzie,' he said bitterly. 'I had believed there was honesty between us if nothing else. Obviously I was proved wrong,' he added harshly, very aware of just how wrong he had been.

Kenzie had lied to him, had deceived him with another man—with Jerome Carlton, a man who had taken great delight in *not* lying to Dominick when he had confronted the other man over the affair. Both of them had made a fool of him. And that was something Dominick simply couldn't allow to go unchallenged.

He was so hard, so implacable, Kenzie realized achingly as she looked at Dominick's unyielding expression. Had he always been this way? Possibly. Except in the past that hard implacability hadn't been directed at her. But now it most assuredly was.

She sighed. 'I don't think discussing the past solves anything, Dominick—'

'I agree,' he said brusquely, straightening. 'We should forget dinner this evening and discuss the arrangements for this weekend now.' His tone was completely businesslike. 'I'll call at your apartment for you at three o'clock on Saturday afternoon. You can expect to be away until Sunday.'

Kenzie gave a pained frown. 'But—I haven't— exactly where are we going, Dominick?'

He shrugged. 'I don't think you really need to know that—'

'Oh, yes, I do,' she assured him forcefully.

He raised his dark brows. 'Frightened that I might hide the body where no one can find it?' he taunted.

Kenzie stood up impatiently. 'You're being ridiculous now—'

'Am I?' He looked across at her carefully. 'Haven't you realized yet, Kenzie, that no one crosses me and just walks away?'

She felt a shiver of apprehension down her spine. 'It's been four months, Dominick—'

'I'm well aware of how long it's been, Kenzie,' he said grimly.

Kenzie looked at him in frustration, wishing for just a glimpse of the softer, more indulgent Dominick that she had seen during their marriage, and on occasion during last weekend at her parents' house. She knew the latter, at least, had all been an act for her family's benefit, an act that had put her totally in Dominick's debt. If Dominick felt any emotion towards her at all now, it was hate.

But he had given her a weekend, and now she owed him a weekend in return...

She drew in a determined breath. 'What sort of clothes will I need to bring with me?'

He shrugged nonchalantly. 'Something to wear for Saturday evening. A swimming costume, perhaps. Or not,' he added throatily as he moved his gaze deliberately down the length of her body.

Kenzie withstood his examination with a determined rise of her chin, although she was a little puzzled as to where he could be taking her if she was going to need an evening dress and a swimming costume—the two didn't seem to go together somehow.

'Dominick, I know you accompanied me to the wedding last weekend, but I really don't think I'm up to a weekend being social with business acquaintances of yours.'

His mouth twisted humourlessly. 'I assure you, Kenzie, the only person you're going to be social with this weekend is me.'

Kenzie was more puzzled than ever. But at the same time she could see by his uncompromising expression that Dominick didn't intend telling her any more than he already had.

'Okay, Dominick, if that's the way you want it,' she agreed abruptly.

'It is.' He nodded.

'I'll leave you to get back to your—work, then,' she said dryly, aware that he hadn't been working at all when she had entered his office uninvited a few minutes ago, but staring out of the window instead.

'And I'll leave you to get back to yours." He gave a mocking inclination of his head. 'Oh, and, Kenzie…?' he added as she reached the door.

She turned back reluctantly. 'Yes?' she prompted warily.

'Enjoy your dinner this evening,' he said softly.

Kenzie searched his face for several long seconds, but once again Dominick made sure she could read nothing from his mocking expression as he steadily returned her gaze.

'Three o'clock on Saturday,' she repeated firmly before making good her escape.

All the humour left Dominick's face once he was alone, his breath leaving him in a shuddering sigh.

Four months since they parted, Kenzie had said.

The same four months it had taken for him to devise

a suitable retribution that would include Kenzie as well as her lover. But it was all coming together now, and it would very shortly be over.

The fact that Kenzie had amazingly come to him last week, needing something from him that only he, as her husband, could give, and therefore putting her totally in his debt, only added to his feelings of satisfaction.

He would take settlement this weekend slowly and leisurely, knowing every caress and pleasure that made Kenzie wild and wanton in his arms. It was a pleasure he intended drinking to the full, a pleasure that would be all the sweeter to him when she returned to her lover after the weekend knowing that she had come to him willingly.

Then Jerome would no doubt inform her of exactly what retribution Dominick had taken on both of them.

Now Dominick waited until he was sure Kenzie had passed through the outer office before sitting forward to press the intercom on his desk. 'Stella, put a call through to Caroline Carlton in New York, will you?' he instructed before sitting back to wait for the connection, his smile of satisfaction not reaching the hard determination of his eyes as he resumed his sightless staring out of the window.

CHAPTER NINE

DOMINICK gave Kenzie a glance from behind dark sunglasses on Saturday afternoon as he drove them to their destination, having picked her up from her apartment almost an hour ago.

As usual Kenzie looked stunningly beautiful as she sat beside him in the car dressed in an emerald-green sundress and high-heeled sandals, the thin straps of the dress showing off her bare shoulders and the creamy swell of her breasts, and her deep green eyes hidden behind the shield of her own sunglasses.

Yes, Kenzie looked stunningly beautiful—and extremely remote, he thought, realizing that since her initial greeting she hadn't spoken a single word.

Now who was the one playing games? Dominick wondered with a hard grin as he returned his attention to the road in front of him. It felt good knowing how easily he could break her cool control.

He decided to do exactly that. 'How was your dinner with Carlton on Wednesday evening?' he enquired mildly, immediately sensing Kenzie's sudden tension.

Kenzie turned to look at him for several long, probing

seconds. 'Why do you ask, when you can't possibly be interested?' she finally sighed.

'Oh, but I am, Kenzie,' Dominick assured her lightly. 'Did you and Carlton have an emotional reunion?' His voice had hardened perceptibly.

'As it happens, we didn't have a reunion of any kind,' she bit out. 'Jerome had to cancel his trip for a couple of days,' she explained as Dominick seemed to be waiting for her to say something else.

'Something more important came up, obviously,' he drawled derisively.

Jerome had telephoned her late on Wednesday to cancel their dinner engagement in the evening, explaining that he had to delay his arrival in England until Saturday because of a pressing business matter that prevented him leaving New York at the moment.

As his dinner with her had also been a business engagement Kenzie hadn't been particularly concerned, the two of them making arrangements to meet on Monday instead once Kenzie had explained she would be away over the weekend. She hadn't told Jerome whom she was going away with though; despite what Dominick chose to believe to the contrary, her private life really wasn't any of Jerome Carlton's business.

'I guess it did,' she acknowledged dismissively.

'Poor Kenzie,' Dominick murmured. 'I seem to remember you accused me of putting business first, too,' he reminded her as she looked at him with a frown.

Kenzie didn't even qualify that remark with an answer; her relationship with Jerome was nothing like her marriage to Dominick, so there was no point in comparing the two.

'Are we nearly there?' she asked instead, the last

hour having taken them out of London and into the Hampshire countryside.

'Not long now,' Dominick confirmed with satisfaction, wondering what Kenzie was going to make of Bedforth Manor. Not that it really mattered; she would never be going there again. But it would still be interesting to see her reaction.

She looked more puzzled than ever when he turned the car into the long gravel, tree-lined driveway that led up to the house, and turned to look at him in confusion as he parked the car in front of the three-storey, mellow-stoned building.

'Bedforth Manor,' he told her economically as he got out of the car to get their bags.

Kenzie followed him slowly, coming to stand beside him at the bottom of the steps that led up to the huge front door. 'Is it a hotel?' she asked.

'If it were it would be a very empty one!' He looked around them pointedly at the lack of any other vehicles in sight.

'But—'

'It's just a house, Kenzie. My house,' Dominick cut in tersely as he began to walk up the steps.

'Yours?' She followed him up the steps feeling slightly dazed.

'Mine,' Dominick turned to assure her.

To say she was surprised was an understatement. Not that Dominick didn't have homes all over the world, but they were mainly apartments, places that could be closed up when Dominick left and then opened up again when he returned possibly months later. A house, at least a house like this one rather than his villas in the

South of France and on his Caribbean island, was something else entirely.

It seemed entirely too permanent a home for a man like Dominick, who made a point of avoiding commitment...

Dominick could see the puzzlement on Kenzie's face, and could guess the reason for it. But he had no intention of telling her that he had originally bought this house for her, and that six months ago he had wanted to at least give her the home she so longed for.

Six months ago, when she was his wife, materially he would have given her almost anything she wanted.

Before she had betrayed him with another man!

He wasn't quite sure why he hadn't just resold the place after she'd left him, because once Kenzie had gone he certainly no longer had any intention of doing it up and living in it.

But he was glad he hadn't got rid of it now; it seemed only poetic justice that he should bring Kenzie here, to the house that he had bought for her but which she would now never live in with him.

A house he probably *would* sell after this weekend...

'I—it's lovely,' she told him in astonishment as he opened the front door and they stepped inside the cavernous hallway.

Dominick looked around him with satisfaction, seeing that the housekeeper had followed the instructions he had given her over the telephone yesterday. There were flowers on the polished table in the centre of the magnificent hallway, their perfume strong and welcoming, and no doubt their dinner was in the kitchen and ready to be cooked. He was sure the master bedroom upstairs had also been prepared for their use...

That housekeeper having now left the house, also as per Dominick's instructions, meant that he and Kenzie were completely alone here.

He really had been speaking the truth when he'd assured her she wouldn't have to be social with anyone but him this weekend!

'Why don't you go through to the kitchen and make us some coffee…' He nodded in the direction of the room straight ahead of him '…while I take our bags upstairs?'

Kenzie was looking around, loving the panelled walls and polished wood floors, the chandelier and wall lights shimmering crystal, and the lovely wide staircase leading up to the second floor. She was so surprised by the house he had brought her to instead of the cold, impersonal hotel she had been expecting that she couldn't even think of an argument to his suggestion as she made her way slowly to the kitchen.

The sort of beautiful old-fashioned kitchen she would have loved for her own, a deep green Aga its dominating feature, pots and pans hanging down over a table scored by years of use, with the more modern features like the fridge and dishwasher hidden away behind doors of the same oak as the array of kitchen cabinets.

Why on earth had Dominick, of all people, bought a beautiful old house like this one?

And where were all the staff needed to run such a big house? she suddenly wondered.

Surely a cook was necessary, if nothing else. Or did Dominick include feeding him as part of the weekend she owed him?

Not that she couldn't cook, in fact she enjoyed it, but despite Dominick's warning that the only person she would have to socialize with this weekend was him, she hadn't for a moment thought that the two of them would be completely alone.

'No coffee?' He raised his dark brows in question as he joined her in the kitchen to find her just standing there. 'Never mind, we'll make some in a minute,' he dismissed. 'Perhaps you would like to have a look at the swimming pool first?'

Somewhere in this big, beautiful house was a swimming pool?

Well, why not? Dominick might not have made anywhere his permanent home the last twenty years, but that didn't mean that he didn't have every comfort in the numerous houses he did own.

'Why not?' She shrugged, needing time to collect her scattered thoughts, and a tour around the swimming pool was as good a way to spend them as any.

'The rose garden,' Dominick told her economically as they went outside. 'The stables.' He pointed over to the buildings some distance away from the house. 'The swimming pool,' he said with satisfaction as he took a key from his pocket and unlocked a door.

Surely swimming pool was too mundane a description of the domed building he took her into, she thought, gazing at the huge windows along each side, the big glass doors at the end wall that opened out onto a terrace, and the full-length pool lined with white and blue mosaics. The pool was surrounded by alabaster pillers, and Greek statues of partially dressed women, set amongst huge urns of overflowing flowers.

'Someone else's fantasy, not mine,' Dominick drawled dryly as Kenzie turned slowly to look at him.

She could have guessed that; she didn't think this romantic setting was Dominick's taste at all.

But it was hers, she realized, the warm enchantment of the place definitely appealing to her. So much so that she longed to get her costume from her bag upstairs and immerse herself in the lovely cool water.

But not if that was going to mean Dominick joining her!

She was already aware of Dominick enough as it was, and had been so since the moment she had joined him in the car earlier. The darkness of his hair had still been damp from the shower he must have taken, his jaw clean-shaven, his muscled arms bare beneath the black polo shirt he wore, and his legs long in the black fitted denims.

Just looking at him had been enough to put all her senses on alert.

And that awareness had only deepened during the journey down here, an emotion she had hopefully kept hidden behind her dark sunglasses.

She drew in a ragged breath. 'Perhaps we should go and have that coffee now?' she prompted quietly, finding this setting far too—intimate, for comfort.

Dominick deliberately put his hand beneath her elbow on the pretext of helping her up the steps as they walked back to the house, and was rewarded by her huskily indrawn breath and the sudden stiffness of her arm before she pulled sharply away from him to walk several feet away.

He smiled to himself as her actions told him that, although Kenzie might try to deny it, even to herself, she still obviously desired him…

'Only trying to be helpful,' he said with a shrug.

He set about preparing the coffee himself once they reached the kitchen, and Kenzie was no longer able to hide her eyes behind dark glasses now that they were back inside the house. Her green eyes looked at him beneath her long, lowered lashes as she sat at the kitchen table watching him fill the coffee machine and set it on to percolate.

'I hope you're going to be more helpful when it comes to preparing dinner,' he rebuked mockingly as he got out the mugs. 'As I'm sure you remember, making coffee and warming ready-prepared meals in a microwave is as far as my culinary talents go!'

Kenzie did remember. She also knew that was because until the two of them had married Dominick had either eaten out or had a live-in cook who had prepared his meals when he had been at home. Any of his homes.

'Where's the staff, Dominick?' she probed warily.

'There isn't any,' he said, sounding unconcerned by her enquiry. 'A woman from the village comes in to check on the place, and she put some flowers in vases and brought in some food for this weekend, but other than that there isn't anyone.'

Meaning they were going to be completely alone here this weekend.

Surely flowers in vases and food for the weekend weren't the details Dominick had told her he still had to finalize before confirming this weekend away?

And what were the two of them doing alone here for the weekend, anyway? What—

'Why don't you stop thinking so much and go and take a swim instead, Kenzie?' Dominick cut into her thoughts harshly, his brown eyes hard and glittering. 'And you accused me of having an overactive imagination!' he added with obvious disgust. 'I thought I had assured you I don't take unwilling women to my bed!'

What about willing ones?

Kenzie was fast coming to the conclusion she wasn't unwilling, and that she never would be where Dominick, the man she loved, was concerned.

Dominick had been her husband, the only man she had shared every intimacy with, and the more time she spent in his company, the harder she was finding it to separate that man she'd fallen for from the stranger he should be to her now.

Was this how all the other women she'd read about felt when they had been married to a man and were thinking about sleeping with him again? A certain curiosity? To see if there really was no last vestige of feeling, no hope, left between them?

She stood up abruptly. 'I think I will go and take that swim, if you don't mind.' A plunge into cold water was probably exactly what she needed!

'I was the one to suggest it, so why should I mind?' Dominick shrugged, obviously still deeply annoyed. 'The bedroom is the first door on the left at the top of the stairs,' he called out to her as she turned and hurried from the room.

She was a fool, Kenzie berated herself as she ran up the stairs as if pursued.

Dominick was deliberately tangling her emotions up in knots and enjoying every moment of it, no doubt.

Although she wasn't so sure that was all he was doing when she got to the bedroom and saw the huge four-poster bed that dominated the room. A huge king-size four-poster bed, with both their weekend bags sitting on top of the brocade cover!

CHAPTER TEN

WHEN Dominick entered the pool-house almost an hour later it was to find Kenzie floating on the water on one of the Lilos, her eyes closed as if in sleep, and her hands trailing gracefully in the water.

She had left her hair loose and it drifted in the water behind the Lilo, her body long and lithe in the red bathing costume that was somehow more tantalizing to the senses than a brief bikini could ever have been.

Dominick felt his body harden and pulse just looking at her.

She was beautiful, exquisitely beautiful, and his four months of celibacy only increased the ache he had to explore every inch of that beauty.

He stripped his clothes off with unhurried ease, dropping them to the floor before letting himself noiselessly down into the water. Then he swam across to where Kenzie floated in the deeper end of the pool.

Kenzie was dozing slightly, the calmness of the pool having soothed her, and her dreams were full of Dominick. Memories of being made love to by him, of making love to him in return, of the sure caresses of his hands on her body and on her breasts, trailing down to her ribcage to touch—

She wasn't dreaming!

Her eyes opened wide in alarm as she realized the massaging hand was a reality, and she turned sharply to find Dominick in the water beside her, her sudden movement stilling his hand.

The emotion in the darkness of his eyes was unmistakable.

It was the same emotion that was suddenly coursing through her.

Desire.

Hot.

Burning.

Immediate!

Dominick saw, and easily recognized, the sudden flare of awareness in Kenzie's gaze.

A gaze that seemed to caress as she looked at the broad expanse of his bare chest before one of her hands moved and her fingers stroked along the path of her vision slowly down his already sensitized flesh.

He groaned low in his throat, his eyes closing as she touched him, opening again at her indrawn breath when her fingers reached his lower stomach and discovered his nakedness.

'Dominick…?' she breathed huskily, looking startled.

'Not now, Kenzie,' he groaned achingly as he reached out and lifted her up into his arms. 'This isn't the time for talking!' he stated forcefully as he carried her towards the shallow end of the pool.

He was right, this moment was too fragile, too immediate for either of them to be able to bring it to a halt.

Dominick stood her in the water, holding her gaze fixedly with his as he peeled the costume down and off her body before sitting her on the side of the pool, standing thigh-high in the water, moved to stand between her legs, before his mouth hungrily claimed hers.

Kenzie matched his appetite, her arms up about his shoulders as lips and tongues demanded each from the other, Dominick's hardness pressed against her own moist heat, hard and yet silken at the same time as he moved rhythmically against her but didn't enter.

Her legs parted further, inviting, her neck arching as his lips travelled the length of her throat, and his hands moved to cup her bared breasts as Kenzie pushed herself into him. She wanted more! So much more!

Dominick altered his position slightly, his head lowering to capture one of her aching nipples in his mouth. Licking it with his tongue, he paused to look up at her. 'Aren't you going to tell me to stop, Kenzie?' he murmured urgently. 'To tell me you don't want this as much as I do?'

She couldn't do it, she thought, she was completely aroused, and her only reply was a low groan in her throat as she offered her breast to him once more.

His eyes glittered darkly as he looked at her, forcing her to watch as he bent his head again, so she could witness, not just feel, the tip of his tongue slowly running over the hardened tip of her breast, before he drew it into his mouth once more.

Kenzie was mesmerized as she watched him pleasuring her. Licking, then gently sucking until she groaned with need and he finally sucked hard against her. Her eyes closed as she arched against him, moist warmth flooding between her thighs, urging for his full possession, wanting the release only Dominick had ever given her.

Then Dominick moved back slightly to run one of his hands between them, down towards her moistness, his thumb then pressing lightly at the core of her desire. He was rewarded by her low whimper as his fingers stroked and caressed, before entering her.

Her warmth closed about him and he began to move inside her, her nipple harder than ever in his mouth, more aroused than ever as her climax began to spiral out of control.

He lifted his head, his hand moving from between them.

'Dominick…?' Kenzie groaned low in protest, the cold air like a caress against her breasts in sharp contrast to the fire that raged between her thighs.

He couldn't leave her now. Couldn't leave her like this. He couldn't!

He didn't.

Instead he knelt in the warmth of the water to kiss his way down to her navel, pausing there for his tongue to tip into the sensual well he found there, his hands on her hips as he plundered.

Kenzie's back was arched, and her hands flat resting on the tiled floor, as she thought how she never wanted these sensations to stop, wanting it all, wanting Dominick.

She wanted him inside her. She wanted him to take her, take them both, to the release that had built so fiercely inside her she thought she would go insane if he didn't soon enter her. She felt desperate for those hard caresses that would take them both over the edge.

He moved lower, his breath warm against her as his

fingers traveled down to part her, Kenzie giving a husky cry as she felt his tongue against her, moist and hard, then soft, curling around her, driving her ever closer towards climax.

It began deep, deep inside, like slow motion, moving oh-so-slowly and sweetly, into her thighs, her legs falling wide as she took him closer into her, her cry almost a scream as she began to convulse against him, his tongue continuing to stroke against her, prolonging and deepening the climax as the tears fell softly down her cheeks as she sobbed her pleasure.

Kenzie felt as if she were falling, everything receding, and then she felt strong arms about her, Dominick's arms, as he lifted and carried her, kissing the tears from her cheeks before laying her down on something soft and cool, his body gently covering hers, his knee nudging her legs apart.

Her eyes opened wide, and she saw the wild need on his arrogant features, his hair a dark tangle about his wide shoulders.

She knew that she wanted to give him what he had given her.

She twisted beneath him, pushing him back against the long cushion he had pulled from one of the loungers around the pool, moving so that he lay beneath her as she straddled him.

'Now, Dominick,' she said huskily, triumphantly, as she moved against the silken length of him, watching his face as it flushed with arousal. 'Shall I take you?' she teased. 'Tell me. Do you want to be inside me?'

'You know I do!' he groaned throatily. 'I want to be inside you now!'

'Soon,' she promised as she moved down the length of his body, kneeling between his legs as she ran her tongue the length of him. 'Very soon,' she assured him, hearing his groan as the heat of her mouth closed about him, her fingers featherlight against him.

'Stop, Kenzie!' he cried minutes later, his hands reaching down to grasp her shoulders. 'Stop now before I—' His expression was almost one of pain as she moved to straddle him once again, his dark eyes pleading. 'For God's sake now, Kenzie!' he muttered.

She lowered herself slowly, very slowly, all the time holding his fevered gaze with hers as he filled her, her own body slick and welcoming as it closed around him.

'Damn it, you're enjoying this!' he groaned throatily.

'Aren't you?' she encouraged as she moved her hips ever so slightly against him, feeling him surge into her as she did so.

'Oh, yes,' he admitted, in rhythm to the thrusts of her body against his, his eyes wide and dark. 'Give me your breast, Kenzie,' he cried wildly.

She leant forward, her hands either side of his head as she lowered her nipple into his mouth, gasping as he drew it deeply inside. He thrust into her at the same time, and the rhythm of their thighs became stronger, fiercer until the pleasure engulfed them, heated them to molten lava, Kenzie taking everything Dominick had to give, and giving the same in return.

She collapsed weakly onto his chest, his arms about her as his heart beat loudly beneath her, their breathing ragged, their bodies still joined.

Their lovemaking had always been fantastic, but this—this had been—

'That was—incredible!' Dominick murmured.

That was the word she had been looking for!

Incredible. Beyond anything they had ever shared before.

Did that mean—? Could it possibly mean that Dominick might feel something for her after all?

'Kenzie…?' he prompted as she lay limply above him, only the even tenor of her breathing telling him that she had recovered much quicker than he had, and that the sharp brain behind her beautiful face and body was already hard at work, dissecting, rationalizing. 'Kenzie, stop analysing!' he rasped as he moved to lay beside her on the cushion, lifting her chin so that she looked at him. 'Just accept this for what it was!' he bit out forcefully. 'Don't put one of your pretty labels on it!'

He wasn't sure what it was himself yet, only that what he had just shared with Kenzie had been unlike anything that he had ever known before, with her or anyone else. The pleasure had been so intense, and the sheer joy of their possession so intimate, so complete, it was beyond description.

What the hell had just happened?

Fourteen months ago he had wanted Kenzie enough to marry her, and he hadn't been disappointed. Taking Kenzie to bed had been as good as he had thought it would be and that had never changed. In fact, he hadn't wanted to have sex with anyone else since he'd met her.

But this, what had happened just now, was something else entirely. It had knocked him totally off his feet and turned his brain to mush, leaving him dazed and incoherent.

Kenzie had actually cried with pleasure!

What did it mean?

It didn't mean anything, he told himself determinedly as he moved abruptly away from her, standing up to begin putting on his clothes.

This was what he had brought Kenzie here for. Sex. Just sex. And that was all it had been.

Kenzie had been with another man for five months, he reminded himself scathingly. She had been sharing Jerome Carlton's bed, and that was why just now had been different. It was because Kenzie was different; she had learnt new and exciting ways to arouse, to give pleasure. At the end she had taken him, for God's sake!

The cold knot of anger that had hardened inside him the last four months turned to ice as he imagined her with Jerome Carlton in the way she had just been with him.

Giving him none of the satisfaction he had thought to find after bending Kenzie to his will.

'Dominick…?'

He looked down at her now, fully dressed while she still lay naked and wanton on the cushion, her hair a dark tangle, her body still warm and beautiful. 'Put some clothes on, Kenzie,' he scorned harshly. 'Play time is over for now. I would like to go back up to the house and eat.'

Kenzie stared at him. He wanted food now? After what had just happened?

But what had really happened?

Dominick had come down to the pool, discovered her half naked, and decided to complete the process, to take what he had always considered his, as he had been warning her for the last week he would do.

The fact that it had been such intense pleasure for her, so much more than ever before, urging her on to behave in a way she never had before, didn't mean that it had been the same for Dominick.

In fact, if his demand for food was anything to go by then she was sure that it hadn't been the same for him!

'You see, Kenzie, it wasn't in my bed at all,' he said, breaking into her tortuous thoughts. 'And, as we both know, you were far from unwilling!' he added with husky mockery.

She briefly felt the hot tears of humiliation, before anger took over, her overbright eyes burning like twin emeralds of fire in the pallor of her face as she got lithely to her feet, totally uncaring of her nakedness.

She was intent now only on hurting him as he was deliberately hurting her. 'I wasn't the one who begged— Let me go, Dominick!' she breathed raggedly as he grasped her arms to pull her hard against him, her face only inches away from his now as he looked down at her coldly, his breath warm against her skin.

He thrust her roughly away from him, hands clenched at his sides, a nerve pulsing in his rigidly clamped jaw. 'Get some clothes on and then come back up to the house,' he grated. 'Our weekend isn't over yet.'

It was as far as Kenzie was concerned!

And there was nothing that Dominick could do or say that was going to make her stay here with him any longer than it took her to dress, collect her bag, and then go!

CHAPTER ELEVEN

KENZIE dressed and tidied her appearance as best she could before returning to the house, breathing an inward sigh of relief when she discovered Dominick wasn't in the kitchen as she had expected he would be.

Although she wasn't quite so lucky as she walked through the main house with the intention of going up to her bedroom to get her bag before leaving.

'Drink?' Dominick growled as she passed the doorway to the sitting room, holding up the glass of brandy he was obviously enjoying.

Kenzie entered the room slowly. It was a beautiful gold and cream room, and the early evening sunshine shining in through the huge bay windows should have looked warm and welcoming, but failed to succeed when it was being dominated by the presence of the tall, darkly brooding man standing beside the unlit fireplace.

Kenzie eyed him in challenge. 'Am I going to need one?'

His mouth twisted humourlessly. 'Probably,' he drawled calmly, moving to the drinks cabinet to pour a second brandy before putting it down on the coffee-table that stood in front of the sofa.

Either Dominick no longer wanted to touch her again, even accidentally, or this was a move on his part to force her to sit down on the gold-coloured sofa, the fact of her having to look up at him instantly putting her on the defensive.

She would take a guess on it being the latter!

Kenzie moved to pick up the glass before strolling over to stand in front of one of the windows, her back to the garden, and the sun streaming in behind her putting her face into shadow.

She hadn't rushed to return to the house, and had taken some time to try to think how she was going to get away. She had tried to decide how she would deal with Dominick if she didn't manage to leave without seeing him again, knowing that her uninhibited response to him in the pool-house had put her at a definite disadvantage.

It was a disadvantage she intended taking back if she could.

'I believe I did try to warn you that statistically those sort of—experiments, never work out,' she reminded him before taking a sip of her brandy, her gaze remaining unwaveringly on his.

Dominick studied her through narrowed lids, filled with the need to hurt and kiss her at the same time!

To hurt her because he couldn't stand the thought of her making love to a man like Jerome Carlton in the way she just had with him. To kiss her because that once hadn't been enough. Not nearly enough!

Instead he looked at her coldly. 'Obviously not,' he

agreed icily, enjoying the angry flush that suddenly coloured her cheeks.

She hadn't liked him saying that. Good. Because he wasn't enjoying himself, either.

And he had expected to. During the months since Kenzie had walked out on him, the thought of what was going to happen next had been the driving force behind all of his actions. He had believed that revenge would be sweet, and this added bonus of making love with Kenzie more than he could possibly have hoped for. But the only result of that was that he knew he still wanted her, damn it!

'Better?' he scorned as Kenzie took another sip of her brandy.

Kenzie didn't respond as he had thought she would, her green eyes glittering with anger rather than tears as she met his gaze full on. 'The brandy is excellent,' she bit out coolly.

He had to admire her, Dominick acknowledged grudgingly; after the passion they had shared down in the poolhouse, and his harshness afterwards, he knew Kenzie must be feeling more than a little unsure of herself, but not by so much as a blink of the eye did she reveal that emotion.

Instead she looked tall and self-possessed, and the bitter rage that welled up inside him made him want to wipe that air of confidence off her beautiful face!

'So aren't you curious to know why your boyfriend had to delay his visit to England for a couple of days?' he asked tauntingly.

Kenzie tensed, but only inwardly; after the humiliation Dominick had tried to inflict earlier she had no intention of letting him see how upset she really was.

She had reacted instinctively to Dominick's love-making; she couldn't have denied her response to him even if she had wanted to. How Dominick must be loving that. In fact, his scathing comments afterwards had already shown her that he did. They both knew now exactly how 'unwilling' she hadn't been!

For a while, a very brief while, Dominick had once again been the man she loved, the experienced but considerate lover who had initiated her into all the pleasures of lovemaking. Even though Dominick refused to believe it, he was the only man she had ever made love with.

But the Dominick he had been after their lovemaking, the Dominick he was now, wasn't the man she had fallen in love with.

Had she really thought that their making love would make any difference to Dominick? To the way he felt about her now?

She hadn't been thinking at all, that was the problem. From the first moment Dominick had touched her, she had only been able to feel!

She drew in a controlling breath. 'If by the phrase "boyfriend" you are referring to Jerome—'

'How many other boyfriends do you have, Kenzie?' Dominick mocked, his brown eyes as hard as pebbles, and his mouth a thin, derisive line.

Her cheeks became flushed in spite of herself. For one thing, at forty-two, Jerome was hardly a boy, and for another, he had never been a boyfriend or anything else in the least intimate to her!

'My marriage to you hasn't exactly made me eager to return to the dating circuit!' she told him accusingly. She was sure the same couldn't be said for Dominick; as she knew only too well, he might not believe in love, but he was an extremely sensual man, and had been involved with lots of women before the two of them had met.

His mouth tightened. 'I very much doubt that's the reason for the oversight, Kenzie. I feel sure that Jerome Carlton is no more eager to share you than I was!'

Kenzie breathed her impatience. 'How many times do I have to tell you that I am not, nor have I ever been, involved in an affair with Jerome Carlton?' Her eyes glittered with anger.

Dominick gave an uninterested shrug. 'You're the one that feels that need, Kenzie, not me.'

'And anyway, what do you know about Jerome's delay in coming to England?' she prompted impatiently, sure from his attitude that Dominick did know something.

The scowl disappeared from Dominick's brow as he gave a relaxed smile. 'Quite a lot, as it happens,' he answered easily.

Kenzie swallowed hard. 'And are you going to tell me?'

'I was going to leave it to Carlton to do that—but why not?' Dominick shrugged. 'About two years ago Carlton Cosmetics hit a few financial difficulties, at which point Carlton decided to float forty-nine per cent of the company shares on the open market, retaining thirty-one per cent for himself, and ten per cent to his two siblings, a younger brother and sister.'

Kenzie had met both Adrian and Caroline Carlton. Adrian actually worked for the company, and she had found him as charming as Jerome, whereas Caroline Carlton had no interest in her brothers or the family-run company, and was only concerned with the income she received from it.

Kenzie moistened her lips. 'And?'

He grimaced. 'At a guess I would say that Carlton has spent the last few days running around in ever-decreasing circles trying to work out how he came to lose control of fifty-one per cent of the shares of his own company!'

He watched with satisfaction as the colour drained from Kenzie's cheeks, her eyes darkening to fathomless pits of green glass.

'You—' She swallowed. 'Tell me you aren't the one responsible for that, Dominick!' she gasped in disbelief.

He gave a humourless smile. 'Now what possible reason would I have to lie to you about something like that, Kenzie?'

She stared at him disbelievingly for several long seconds before moving to the sofa and sitting down abruptly, her hands trembling as her fingers curled about the brandy glass.

'I did warn you you might need the brandy,' Dominick said, with a smug look on his face.

Kenzie was breathing shallowly, feeling so stunned she couldn't move or speak. It was incredible to think that for the last four months Dominick had been plotting and scheming—

So *these* were the 'plans' he had still had to finalize on Wednesday!

But why had he done this? He didn't love her; he had never loved her, so why should her leaving him have bothered him in the slightest—even if he did persist in believing she had left him for the arms of another man?

Pride.

She had damaged that Masters pride, and Dominick had taken retribution for it.

But in what a way—!

'I can't believe you did this, Dominick,' she said quietly, shaking her head in disbelief.

Dominick's top lip curled contemptuously. 'If you have any doubts that I'm the person who now owns fifty-one per cent of Carlton Cosmetics, then don't,' he assured her confidently before drinking the remainder of the brandy in his glass, enjoying the smooth burning sensation of the alcohol as it slid down his throat. 'But I'm afraid Carlton only learnt of the takeover very recently when Caroline told him that she had sold her ten per cent of the company shares. To me,' he added with satisfaction. He shrugged impassively, his dark eyes narrowing as he watched Kenzie's reaction.

Pained disbelief. Followed by slow acceptance which quickly turned into an anger that now burned in the depths of her glittering green eyes and the twin spots of colour in her cheeks. She slammed her brandy glass down on the coffee-table before standing up to glare at him.

She shook her head. 'I can't believe that even you could do something so despicable—'

'Even me?' he echoed. 'Careful now, Kenzie. Unless you haven't realized it yet, my shares in Carlton Cosmetics mean that your contract with the company now belongs to me…' he pointed out softly.

Kenzie stared at him for several long, painful seconds, still stunned that Dominick could have deliberately bought control of Carlton Cosmetics. With the help of Caroline Carlton, Jerome's own sister!

Not that the latter altogether surprised her; Caroline never made any secret where her interest in the company lay, and Kenzie didn't doubt that Dominick had made Caroline a very tempting financial offer for her shares.

As for her own contract with Carlton Cosmetics—!

She shook her head. 'I'll never work for you, Dominick.'

'Then I'll have to sue you for breach of contract.'

'My contract is with Jerome.'

'Your contract is with Carlton Cosmetics!' he corrected harshly.

'Of which I am now the majority shareholder.'

It had taken four months of finding out exactly who the shareholders of Carlton Cosmetics were, then cajoling and charming those shareholders into selling to him. Confirmation on Wednesday for the purchase of the last ten per cent from Jerome Carlton's own sister, Caroline, meant Dominick was now in control of the company formerly run by the man who had seduced and bedded his wife. And at the same time he had taken control of the eight months left of Kenzie's year-long contract with the company.

Retribution, indeed!

Kenzie, although still standing tall and proud, was deathly pale now as the full weight of what Dominick was saying hit her with the force of a sledgehammer.

'Then I'm afraid you'll have to sue me, Dominick,' she finally breathed raggedly. 'Because there is no way I will ever work for you! In fact—' she straightened '—after today, after what you've done, I never want to set eyes on you again!'

'Really?' he taunted.

'Yes—really!' she echoed forcefully.

'That might be a little difficult, Kenzie, when I have

every intention of becoming completely involved in all aspects of Carlton Cosmetics,' Dominick stated.

How could Dominick have done this? she wondered in a daze.

Kenzie had known him as many things since she had first met him: as the man she loved; the man she married; the man she couldn't stay with any more because he was incapable of returning her love, and then the deeply angry man who had challenged her to walk away from him.

But the Dominick he was now was consumed with a need for revenge, on Jerome Carlton, and on her, to the extent that he had taken that vengeance by trying to ruin both of them.

She didn't doubt that he had ruined Jerome.

And he would succeed in ruining her too if she refused to continue working for Carlton Cosmetics and he sued her for breach of contract. Something, after today, she was sure he was more than capable of doing!

She gave a disbelieving shake of her head. 'I think I can understand your need to get back at me, Dominick,' she said dully. 'But why you felt it necessary to drag Jerome into your vendetta is totally beyond me—'

'Is it?' he cut in fiercely. 'Then you obviously don't know me very well, Kenzie.'

She looked at him with blank, unemotional eyes. 'I'm beginning to think that I never knew you at all,' she murmured quietly. 'One thing I do know—I'll never forgive you for doing this, Dominick. Never,' she assured him softly before turning away.

'Where are you going?' he called after her harshly.

She glanced back at him with dull eyes. 'Away from here. Away from you,' she said with emphasis.

'Do you really think it's going to be that easy, Kenzie?' he scorned.

Leaving him the first time had been horrible, but leaving the stranger he had become now wasn't difficult at all!

But that wasn't what Dominick meant, of course, his controlling interest of Carlton Cosmetics meaning that if she couldn't break her contract—and Dominick seemed pretty certain that she couldn't!—then for the next eight months, at least, the two of them would be bound together and forced to meet.

She gave him a pitying look. 'Do you know the saddest part of all this, Dominick?' She frowned. 'No, of course you don't,' she answered her own question derisively. 'Your behaviour—what you've done...' She shook her head sadly. 'Oh, I can't deny that the next eight months are going to be difficult—'

'I'm sure you can't,' he rasped.

'But you don't see what you've really done at all, do you, Dominick?' Kenzie sighed. 'No matter what you might believe, until now I've only ever had a working relationship with Jerome, but now, after what you've done to him because of that relationship, you've actually succeeded in uniting the two of us. Against you, if nothing else.'

'That's nothing new,' he dismissed scathingly.

'I feel sorry for you, Dominick,' she whispered. 'I really do.'

'Don't waste your pity,' he advised harshly.

'No,' she accepted heavily, giving him one last sorrowful glance before turning on her heel and leaving the room.

Dominick stood rigidly as he heard her ascent up the

stairs, followed seconds later by the lightness of her step as she came back down again, listening as the front door closed behind her with soft finality as she left the house altogether.

Kenzie was walking out on him for the second time!

Strangely, he felt none of the satisfaction that he had thought, either at having made love to her in the way he had, or on telling her of his controlling interest in Carlton Cosmetics. He could only remember the disgust in her face when she had realized what he had done, and her disbelief.

Her hatred…

Kenzie really did hate him now, he realized as he poured himself another brandy. It had been there in her face as she had looked at him that last time, and in the pained disillusionment in her eyes.

Well, it was what he had wanted, wasn't it—what the last four months, and this weekend, had all been about?

Then why did that cold dish of revenge feel so much like a leaden weight, giving him a sick feeling in the pit of his stomach rather than the fulfilment he had expected to feel…?

CHAPTER TWELVE

WHATEVER Kenzie had expected Dominick's next move to be after that awful day at Bedforth Manor, she was left in suspense for the next five weeks, as the time passed with no word or sight of him.

Not that the silence wasn't a relief. It was just surprising at the same time.

But this evening that was going to come to an abrupt end because tonight was the launch party of Carlton Cosmetics' new fragrance, an event that, as the promotional face of the company, required Kenzie's attendance. She had flown to New York especially for the occasion, and, as she knew from conversations with Jerome, Dominick had every intention of being at the party too.

She and Jerome, united as she had warned Dominick they would be, had consulted with a lawyer to see if there wasn't something to be done about Dominick's stranglehold on Carlton Cosmetics and her own contract with the company. But, as she might already have guessed, there was nothing illegal about Dominick's purchase of the shares, and there was no suitable let-out clause in her

own contract, either—not wanting to work for your es-
tranged husband wasn't reason enough, apparently!

Dominick, with his usual thoroughness, had tied the
company, and her, up in legalities that simply couldn't
be broken.

So they were stuck with it, and Dominick, a fact that,
understandably, didn't sit too well with Jerome.

'The brute should be making his grand entrance any
time soon!'

Jerome muttered as he joined Kenzie near the entrance of the reception room at one of New York's most
prominent hotels. Chandeliers glittered over the elegant
heads of the society guests and members of the media,
and the room was abuzz with conversation and the soft
music being played by a string quartet.

It wasn't too difficult, in the circumstances, to guess
which 'brute' Jerome was referring to!

'Perhaps he'll do us all a favour and decide not to
come, after all,' she dismissed distractedly, totally on
edge as she kept half an eye on the door while she cir-
cuited the room talking and smiling with the other guests.

'We couldn't be that lucky.' Jerome scowled, still
boyishly attractive despite his forty-two years.

But Jerome's looks were such that they had never
appealed to Kenzie. Firstly because when she had met
him she had still been married to Dominick and had had
no interest in other men, and then later simply because
she wasn't attracted to him. As she hadn't been to any
man after she and Dominick had parted…

'Here he comes now,' Jerome announced scathingly.

Kenzie tensed so suddenly that she spilt some of the
champagne from her glass over her fingers, fingers that

gripped the slender stem of the flute so tightly it was in danger of snapping.

'And, damn it, he's brought Caroline with him!' Jerome added angrily.

Kenzie was licking the champagne from her fingers when she turned in time to see cameras snapping as Dominick made his entrance. He looked tall and powerful in his black evening suit, snowy white shirt and red tie—the colour of which exactly matched the clinging red dress Kenzie was wearing, she was totally dismayed to see.

Standing at his side, looking beautifully triumphant, was Caroline Carlton, her blonde hair tumbling loosely over her bare shoulders, and the black shimmering dress she wore clinging to the fullness of her voluptuous figure.

Kenzie hadn't known Dominick was bringing anyone with him this evening—he hadn't deigned to inform anyone what his plans were—but it didn't come as a complete surprise to her that he should have chosen to bring Caroline.

There had been an almighty row between Caroline and her two brothers when they had found out what she had done, resulting in Caroline being banned from coming anywhere near them, or Carlton Cosmetics, ever again.

No doubt it was amusing Dominick greatly to bring the other woman to an event she hadn't been invited to!

'Perhaps we should try to disconcert him and go over and say hello,' she suggested softly, aware that the majority of the guests were now watching them. They were all aware of Dominick's takeover of Carlton Cosmetics—it had been a nine-day wonder in the newspapers a month ago—and they were obviously curious to see what would happen next, the media in particular.

But as there had still been no announcement of the impending divorce between Kenzie and Dominick—he still hadn't signed and returned the papers—none of the press seemed to be aware of any estrangement between the two of them, thank goodness!

Jerome gave her a glowering glance. 'You go over and say hello—I'm going to get myself another drink!' he muttered disgustedly before disappearing into the crowd.

Kenzie closed her eyes briefly. Six and a half more months of her contract, that was all she had to get through—

'You're looking very beautiful this evening, Kenzie,' Dominick whispered huskily as he appeared at her side.

He watched as Kenzie turned to look at him with startled green eyes, her cheeks seeming to pale slightly beneath expertly applied make-up.

Make-up that Dominick knew only too well Kenzie didn't really need, her natural beauty such that it required no enhancement.

She looked amazing in her clinging red dress, her breasts pert, waist slender—perhaps a little more so than he remembered—and her hips were curvaceously sensual. She seemed to stand out in this roomful of 'beautiful people' with the brightness of a shimmering flame, so much so that Dominick had had no trouble in immediately locating her when he had arrived, even as he'd smiled for the cameras that had clicked so annoyingly in his face.

'Champagne?' He offered her one of the two glasses he had carried over with him.

She raised her dark eyebrows at him. 'Shouldn't you be offering that to Caroline?'

He shrugged. 'I believe she has gone over to have a chat with her elder brother.'

Kenzie glanced across the room to where Jerome and Caroline looked to be in the middle of a heated, if muted, conversation. 'Not a pleasant one, by the look of it,' she dismissed coolly, totally ignoring the champagne he offered her. 'Doesn't it bother you that you've caused a total rift in the Carlton family?'

Knowing how important Kenzie's family was to her—important enough for her to have made the bargain with him in the first place!—Dominick could see that being a problem for her, possibly more of one than his usurping Jerome's control over Carlton Cosmetics had been.

'But of course it doesn't bother you,' Kenzie answered her own question dismissively. 'I'm sure it only serves to confirm for you once again the fragility of family relationships!'

Dominick's mouth tightened at the barb. The last five weeks of deliberately staying away from Kenzie hadn't been easy for him, his emotions fluctuating between wanting to see her again and knowing that he was the last person she wanted to see. Something she had made very plain the last time they had been together.

The problem—and it was a problem that had grown greater with each passing day—was that he *wanted* to see Kenzie.

That last time they were together, making love beside the pool at Bedforth Manor, had been earth-shattering for him, and was a memory he hadn't been able to get out of his head.

Kenzie had told him their marriage was over, that she

wanted a divorce, and yet could she have made love to him in the way she had if she felt nothing for him?

More to the point, could he have made love to her in the way he had if he didn't have feelings for her…?

He had always been a man completely in control of his emotions, and yet that day beside the pool he had completely lost that control—and had felt truly alive for the first time in months!

It hadn't helped that, with Kenzie's departure that day, the anger that had burned so dangerously in him for the previous four months seemed to have disappeared, leaving him with a feeling of leaden nausea that refused to go away.

It had always been his intention to actually be present when Jerome Carlton was told that he had lost control of his own company, but after that last conversation with Kenzie, and the look of disappointment and disgust she had given him before she left, he had stayed away rather than have to see that look in Kenzie's face again.

Whatever madness had possessed him after Kenzie had left him five and a half months ago had disappeared now, and in its place was only the realization of Kenzie's hatred, along with the knowledge that in his desire for revenge he had single-handedly destroyed any feelings she might ever have had for him.

All this time he had thought that was what he wanted, only to learn, once Kenzie had left him for good, that having her hate him wasn't what he wanted at all…

No wonder Kenzie had felt sorry for him five weeks ago.

He would feel sorry for himself if he didn't abhor self-pity!

Because he had been the fool, more of a fool than he could ever have guessed. But the realization had come too late!

'I don't think about fragility where your own family is concerned,' he reminded her softly. 'I seem to remember that I agreed to come to Kathy's wedding in order to help you in your effort not to upset or distress your father after his illness…?'

Something flickered briefly in her deep green eyes, something so fleeting that it had come and gone before Dominick had time to analyse it.

'For a price, Dominick,' Kenzie said scathingly.

He frowned darkly at being reminded of that price. 'I'm not responsible for the rift in the Carlton family, either—Caroline's greed is responsible for that.'

Kenzie shrugged. 'No doubt you made her an offer she would have been a fool to refuse!'

Yes, he had. And it was obvious what Kenzie thought of such a manoeuvre.

The self-disgust he felt was as alien to him as the self-pity.

His mouth tightened. 'Carlton could always make *me* an offer I can't refuse and buy them back from me!'

Kenzie gave him a searching glance, finally shaking her head in disbelief. 'Just so that you could have the satisfaction of telling him no? I don't think so, Dominick!'

'Maybe I wouldn't say no.' He shrugged. 'After all, I've achieved what I set out to do—'

'Revenge on Jerome and humiliation for me?' Kenzie cut in harshly, not sure how much longer she could continue this conversation. Her legs had started to feel decidedly shaky, and little flashes of light were dancing in front of her eyes.

It was probably because she'd had nothing to eat today, she thought. She had been too nervous about seeing Dominick again this evening to even contemplate the thought of food, and had actually been physically sick this morning due to her apprehension.

But her shakiness now told her that she should have forced herself to eat something later in the day, because she was definitely in danger of fainting at Dominick's feet.

'I didn't—' Dominick broke off his impatient reply, his brow creasing into a frown as he looked at her closely. 'Kenzie, are you okay?'

'No, I'm not okay,' she answered irritably. 'This situation is even more impossible than I thought it was going to be!'

He could see that by the pallor of her cheeks and the dark shadows beneath her eyes. And she was thinner than when he had seen her five weeks ago...

His frown deepened. 'I think you need something to eat—'

'And I think I just need you to leave me alone!' she told him, agitated.

But he couldn't do that now that he had seen her again, talked to her again. He didn't know how he was ever going to let her walk out of his life again!

'If you'll excuse me, Dominick.' Kenzie grimaced, determined that she wasn't going to collapse; if she fainted at all then she wasn't going to be anywhere near Dominick when she did it!

He reached out to touch her arm. 'Kenzie—'

'I need to go and powder my nose,' she continued

firmly, shaking off his restraining hand. 'You're welcome to join me, of course,' she added derisively as she saw his frowning expression, 'but I think it might look a little odd if you were to follow me into the Ladies' room!'

Instead it was Dominick's gaze that followed her longingly as she moved easily across the room, pausing to talk and smile with several of the other guests as she did so.

An elusive flame not just a shimmering one!

Well, what had he expected?

His behaviour five weeks ago had ensured that Kenzie would never willingly be in his company ever again. In fact, she had told him as much before she had left that day.

But after five agonizing weeks, when he had taken a good hard look at himself—and hadn't liked what he had seen!—he knew that he was getting exactly what he deserved.

Even Kenzie's relationship with Jerome Carlton was no longer so black and white to him as it had once seemed.

Kenzie had told Dominick that she loved him, but it was a love he had told her he was incapable of returning, so maybe it was his own fault she had turned to Jerome Carlton. Maybe *he* was responsible for pushing her into the arms of a man who did love her…?

Except that Dominick didn't believe Jerome Carlton was capable of loving any woman more than he did himself.

Jerome Carlton, he knew from enquiries five and a half months ago, was shallow and vain, and completely ruthless when it came to business—a trait Dominick recognized all too easily. His affairs were legendary, and the end of those affairs, when the woman ceased to be of interest—or use—to him, just as legendary.

But not his affair with Kenzie. At least, not yet…

Kenzie's legs carried her only long enough to get safely inside the powder room before she collapsed down onto the side of the plush red velvet seat that dominated the centre of the elegantly marbled outer room, bending down to put her head between her knees as she felt the waves of nausea washing over her.

This was awful.

She had known tonight was going to be an ordeal, and had thought she'd been prepared for it—well, as prepared as she could be—and yet she knew she was still in danger of making a complete idiot of herself by fainting!

She wouldn't faint. There was no way she would give Dominick that satisfaction.

Nevertheless, it took some minutes for the dizziness to recede enough for her to be able to go over to one of the marble sinks and splash some cold water on her face, Several other women came into the room in the meantime, and Kenzie smiled at their friendly enquiries as she assured them it was just the heat of the reception room that was making her feel slightly light-headed.

She was standing in front of the sink, checking her appearance in front of the mirror, when she saw Caroline Carlton enter the room behind her.

She stiffened slightly before deliberately looking away; the two women had never particularly got on before, and now Kenzie was all too aware that it was Caroline's selling of her shares in Carlton Cosmetics that had put them all in this tenuous position.

Caroline pursed her lips as she joined Kenzie in front of the mirror. 'I suppose you don't like me very much, either,' she mocked nonchalantly as she reached in her bag before replenishing her lipgloss.

Kenzie shrugged her bare shoulders. 'It's really none of my business what you choose to do with your own property, Caroline,' she dismissed lightly, turning away with the intention of returning to the reception room.

'Try convincing my big brother of that!' Caroline muttered disgustedly.

Kenzie gave a rueful smile as she turned back to the other woman. 'I'm afraid I don't have that sort of influence with Jerome.'

Caroline gave a derisive smile. 'That isn't what Dominick thinks!'

Kenzie instantly stiffened. 'Dominick…?' she repeated awkwardly.

'It really is rather greedy of you, Kenzie,' Caroline reproved. 'For months Jerome has been running around granting your every whim, and you obviously still have Dominick enthralled!'

'I don't think so somehow,' Kenzie replied calmly. 'On either count,' she added firmly, a little tired of people making assumptions about her friendship with Jerome. And as for Dominick being 'enthralled' with her…!

'Please yourself,' Caroline drawled, obviously bored with the subject. 'I only came in here to see if you're okay, and you obviously are, so—'

'Why on earth would you care if I'm okay or not?' Kenzie frowned her surprise.

'I don't—but Dominick does,' Caroline informed her

cattily. 'He sent me in here to check on you like I was some errand girl—'

Kenzie didn't hear what Caroline said next as the light-headedness returned with a vengeance, all the colours of the rainbow seeming to dance briefly in front of her eyes before she was engulfed in total blackness.

CHAPTER THIRTEEN

KENZIE felt totally disoriented when she woke up. She didn't recognize the bedroom she lay in and she definitely didn't have any idea how she had come to be here.

But as she began to look around the dimly lit room she did recognize the man standing so tall and forbidding in front of one of the windows as he gazed bleakly over the New York skyline.

'Dominick...?'

Dominick turned sharply at the husky sound of Kenzie's voice, his expression lightening as he moved to sit on the side of the bed. 'No, don't move,' he instructed firmly as she began to push herself up. 'The doctor should be here in a few minutes,' he added with impatience.

'But—'

'Please don't move, Kenzie.' Dominick reached out to lightly grasp her shoulders as he gently pushed her back against the pillows. 'We have no idea what's wrong with you yet, and until we do I think you should just lie still,' he advised softly, instinctively reaching up to smooth her dark hair away from her pale face. His hand dropped away, a nerve pulsing in his tightly clenched jaw, as she just as instinctively moved away from his touch.

She moistened her dry lips. 'What happened? One minute I was talking to Caroline, and the next— Where am I? More to the point, how did I get here?' She frowned her confusion.

'I'm staying in the hotel, so I brought you up to my suite,' Dominick explained before standing up to walk away, still having no idea what was wrong with Kenzie, but very aware that his close proximity wasn't helping her to feel any better. 'As for how you got here, I carried you—'

'But I was in the ladies' powder room when I fainted!' Kenzie protested as memory began to come back to her.

Dominick gave a rueful smile. 'I guess I followed you into the ladies' powder room after all. And you were right about it causing a sensation,' he acknowledged dryly. 'Although the fact that you were unconscious when I carried you out of there was probably the reason for that!' he added grimly.

Kenzie closed her eyes briefly as she easily imagined the commotion that must have caused. So much for wanting everything to run smoothly this evening. Jerome was probably having an apoplectic fit at Dominick having whisked away the face of Carlton Cosmetics in this high-handed way!

'Why on earth did you bring me up to your hotel suite, of all places?' she protested impatiently as she began to sit up.

'I told you to stay put!' Dominick rasped as he came back to the bedside.

Her eyes flashed a dark shade of green as she looked up at him. 'I'm sure you think you acted for the best when you brought me up here, Dominick, but don't let that give you the mistaken impression you have the right to tell me to do anything!'

His mouth tightened. 'Maybe not,' he conceded bitterly.

'Definitely not,' she told him with finality. 'Now, if you will excuse me, I have a job to do—'

'You aren't going anywhere until a doctor has seen you,' Dominick insisted grimly.

Kenzie sat up to swing her legs off the bed and onto the floor. 'I don't need to see a doctor,' she said determinedly. 'I've been—too busy, to eat today, that's all—'

'You mean your anticipation of seeing me again this evening was such that you didn't feel like eating!' Dominick guessed, knowing exactly what that felt like— he hadn't been able to eat today, either. In fact, he couldn't remember when he had last had a decent meal…

Kenzie gave him a scathing glance. 'Don't flatter yourself, Dominick,' she scorned. 'I haven't thought about you enough in the last five weeks to care one way or the other,' she added coldly.

'No?' he sneered to hide the fact that her barb had hit home—he had thought of nothing *but* her for the last five weeks!

'No!' she said firmly. 'Now, if you wouldn't mind getting out of my way I need to go back downstairs to try to repair some of the damage you did with your heroics earlier—'

'You would rather I had just left you on the damned floor, is that it?' he grated impatiently.

'I believe I told you I would rather you just stayed

away from me altogether!' she snapped. 'Go and find Caroline—I'm sure she will be more than happy to see you!'

'Caroline…?' Dominick frowned. 'What the hell does Caroline have to do with anything?'

'You came with her, didn't you?' Kenzie reminded him, with a scowl.

'She came with me,' Dominick corrected. 'She telephoned me earlier today and asked if she could.'

'Really?'

'Yes—really!' he confirmed in frustration as he ran a hand through the dark thickness of his hair.

'And you were only too pleased to say yes!' Kenzie accused.

'No, I—' he broke off impatiently. 'What the hell does it matter to you who I came here with, Kenzie?'

Yes, why did it matter to her? Kenzie asked herself.

Seeing Dominick again, and talking to him, had shown her that her feelings for him weren't dead, after all. They were only hidden in the dark recesses of her heart where they couldn't hurt her any more. Where Dominick couldn't hurt her any more.

Over the past few weeks, she had channelled all her emotions into remembering the anger and disappointment she had felt for Dominick when they had parted, but all that had changed when she had seen him arrive here this evening with Caroline Carlton…

She had been jealous of that other woman clinging so intimately to his arm!

Caroline Carlton, of all women.

A woman she had never liked. A woman she would never like now.

But it was still jealousy. After all that had happened, after all the pain they had deliberately inflicted on each other, she still loved Dominick, and that was why it mattered to her that he had come with someone else.

'It doesn't,' she lied. 'I just thought you might have had better taste, that's all.'

Dominick glowered at her. 'I am not, nor have I ever been, involved with Caroline Carlton—'

'I told you, it's of no interest to me if you are!'

'It doesn't sound that way to me!'

'I don't care how it sounds to you—' She broke off as a knock sounded on the outer door.

'That will be the doctor now,' Dominick growled. 'At least let him examine you now he's here.'

She could do that, yes, Kenzie conceded, dropping weakly back against the pillows as Dominick left the bedroom to go through to the sitting room to answer the door. She felt as drained by the argument they had just had as much as by her faint earlier.

Mainly because, in all honesty, she still felt extremely light-headed, and it would only have been sheer stubbornness on her part that would have got her on her feet and back downstairs.

But she was pretty sure the doctor was going to tell her that it was tension and lack of food today that had caused her to faint, so there really was no reason for Dominick to look quite so grim as the doctor came into the room and began to ask her questions.

'Dominick, would you mind going into the other room?' she requested coolly as the doctor expressed his wish for a more thorough examination.

Yes, he did mind, damn it, Dominick acknowledged with a scowl.

Kenzie could have no idea of his shock earlier, and his feelings of concern when Caroline Carlton had come running out of the powder room to tell him Kenzie had collapsed.

Nor had Kenzie seen the gentleness with which Dominick had gathered her up in his arms, harshly brushing away Jerome Carlton's questions when he had emerged into the crowded reception room seconds later with Kenzie still cradled against him. She hadn't seen him stride forcefully towards the lift while he barked an order at the flustered hotel manager to call a doctor and have him sent up to his suite as soon as he arrived.

She had looked so pale when Dominick had carried her along the corridor to his hotel room, her long dark hair trailing over his arm adding to that air of fragility. Kenzie had seemed to weigh nothing in his arms despite her tall stature.

So, yes, he did mind leaving the room because he wanted to know what the hell was wrong with her!

'I think it might be as well if your husband stayed, Mrs Masters,' the doctor told her with a smile. He was a short iron-grey-haired man who was obviously slightly in awe of Dominick glowering across the room at him.

Kenzie's face regained some of its colour. 'He's not—'

'I'll go and stand by the other window if it makes you more comfortable, Kenzie,' Dominick cut in on what he knew was going to be her protest at having him called her husband let alone finding herself addressed as Mrs Masters.

But that was exactly what she still was, he brooded as he moved to the other end of the bedroom, totally deaf to the murmur of Kenzie and the doctor's voices.

Kenzie was Mrs Masters whether she liked it or not. His wife. As he was still her husband.

He had taken the divorce papers out of his desk drawer a dozen times over the last five weeks, not with the intention of signing and returning them, but as a way of reminding himself that, no matter how much he might have changed, Kenzie no longer wanted anything more to do with him.

He was vaguely aware now of Kenzie going into the bathroom, then returning a couple of minutes later, and the low whisper of voices as the doctor spoke to her again.

'Well, I believe that's perfectly in order,' the doctor said as he straightened and turned to include Dominick in his smile. 'Nothing to worry about at all, Mr Masters—'

'Kenzie collapsed, so of course I'm worried,' Dominic snapped.

'Your wife only fainted, Mr Masters,' the doctor assured him as he packed his things away in his bag. 'It's perfectly common at this stage of things, I do promise you. Of course, Mrs Masters will need to see her own doctor as soon as possible, and if these fainting spells continue I'm sure he will be—'

'What-is-wrong-with-her?' Dominick interrupted tautly, his patience having been tested beyond endurance.

'I believe congratulations are in order,' the older man beamed. 'Your wife is in the early stages of pregnancy.'

Pregnant…?

Kenzie was *pregnant!*

CHAPTER FOURTEEN

'I HAVE the distinct feeling,' Dominick murmured as he returned to the bedroom after seeing the doctor out and found Kenzie glaring at him from across the room, 'that if I were to even dare to question the paternity of your baby at this moment I might end up with more than I bargained for!'

'Your feeling is correct!' Kenzie bit out between gritted teeth, not even close to coming to terms with her pregnancy.

It hadn't even occurred to her—

She hadn't thought—

She was expecting the baby she had so longed for six months ago!

Dominick's baby…

That realization was enough to take her breath away. In fact, she was surprised she hadn't fainted all over again when the doctor had announced his prognosis.

Pregnant.

But not, as she had always dreamt, within the confines of a close and happy marriage. She and her baby's father didn't even live together any more, and would be divorced as soon as possible after Dominick signed the papers.

She really was pregnant. With Dominick's baby. And while it was something he didn't want or need, Kenzie knew that she would love this baby enough for both of them.

'I have no idea what you're thinking now, Kenzie,' Dominick said gruffly as he watched the emotions flickering across her face. 'Although I could take a pretty fair guess!' he added ruefully. 'But whatever it is, I think we should hold off discussing—any of this, until after you've had something to eat.'

Inwardly Dominick wasn't quite as calm. In fact, he had no idea what he was.

Kenzie was pregnant!

With his baby?

Or was it Carlton's?

His heart constricted at that thought. 'I'll go through to the other room and order you some food while you put a call through to your parents—'

'It's far too early to tell them of the pregnancy yet,' Kenzie instantly protested. She hadn't got used to the idea herself yet, let alone sharing it with the rest of her family.

Dominick grimaced. 'I wasn't suggesting that you tell your family about the pregnancy,' he assured dryly. 'After your collapse earlier, and all those snap-happy reporters downstairs as I carried you up here, your parents may find some of the headlines in tomorrow's newspapers a little—disturbing. It may be as well if you were to call them before that happens to let them know that you're okay.'

Kenzie stared at him for several long seconds, surprised that he had even considered how her parents might feel.

'Okay,' she finally agreed quietly, feeling wary of Dominick in this mood.

Where was the Dominick she knew who wouldn't have hesitated to make accusations and recriminations?

Maybe it was just that he was as stunned as she was.

'Is a club sandwich okay or would you prefer something more substantial?' he enquired with that same calm she was finding so disturbing.

'A club sandwich will be fine,' she answered slowly.

'With coffee or juice? I really have no idea whether pregnant women are supposed to drink coffee or not.' He grimaced.

'Juice will be fine,' Kenzie murmured, still eyeing him with unease.

He nodded. 'I shouldn't be long. If you would like to call your parents…?' he reminded her before disappearing into the adjoining sitting room.

Kenzie stood rooted to the spot for several seconds after Dominick had left, still puzzled by his behaviour.

Five months ago, even five weeks ago, she would have had no doubts as to his reaction on learning she was pregnant, and would have known exactly how he felt about the prospect of fatherhood. Now she had no idea what he was thinking or feeling.

But that was probably because he didn't know whether the baby was his or not, she instantly reasoned. Why should he? The two of them had made love once in the last five and a half months, whereas he thought she and Jerome were virtually living together.

That had to be the answer to his odd behaviour; Dominick wasn't sure whose baby she was expecting.

Whereas she knew it couldn't be anyone else's but his!

Which put her in a precarious position. Did she tell Dominick the baby was his? Or did she let him go on thinking she might be pregnant by another man?

Whichever she decided to do, one thing she was sure of: Dominick wouldn't *want* this baby to be his!

As Dominick put through the order for Kenzie's food, his mind was whirring with questions.

He and Kenzie had made love five weeks ago, so depending on how pregnant Kenzie was, it could be his baby.

How did he feel about that?

He had no idea how he felt about the baby itself, and couldn't even begin to quantify or rationalize emotions about something so far beyond his comprehension, but the thought of Kenzie being pregnant with his child was something else entirely…

If it was his baby—and it was a big if, he acknowledged grimly—then he wanted to be there for her, by his physical presence and support, financially, or in any way she would let him be there for her.

The question was, would *she* want him to be there for any of those things…?

'Are your parents okay?' he queried evenly, returning to the bedroom to find Kenzie sitting on the side of the bed beside the telephone.

She turned to him blankly, having been lost in thought. 'Fine,' she dismissed quickly as she stood up.

Get a grip, Kenzie, she told herself firmly; there would be plenty of time to think of the enormity of what was happening to her once she was alone later tonight.

'How is your father now?' Dominick asked lightly.

'Much better,' she answered a little impatiently.

'Dominick, if you want to start hurling out those accusations now, it's okay. I'm feeling less—stunned, than I was a few minutes ago,' she assured him wryly.

'I don't—' He shook his head, his face slightly pale beneath his tan. 'I have no idea what to say,' he finally acknowledged.

He knew that whatever he said in the next few minutes it was sure to be wrong!

'That has to be a first,' Kenzie murmured ruefully.

He shrugged. 'All of this is a first for me.'

'But you do want to know whether or not the baby is yours?' Kenzie questioned.

Did he?

He wasn't sure what he wanted. If Kenzie told him the baby definitely wasn't his, then there would be no going back from that. Carlton was sure to want his baby, as well as Kenzie, and Dominick would have lost her for ever.

Whatever else their time together five weeks ago, and seeing her this evening had shown him, it was that he could no longer stand the thought of losing her. He couldn't bear the thought of never being able to hold her, to talk to her, to laugh with her, ever again!

'Don't look so worried, Dominick,' Kenzie derided as she saw his expression. 'Whether or not this baby is yours, it isn't going to affect you in the slightest—'

'Don't be so damned stupid, Kenzie!' he rasped impatiently, thrusting his hands into his trouser pockets as he began to pace the room. 'Of course it will affect me. It would be my son or daughter, for God's sake!' He frowned darkly.

She raised her dark brows. 'And that would bother you?'

'Of course it would bother me!' He paused to glare at her. 'Admittedly fatherhood isn't something I ever thought about—'

'Or wanted,' Kenzie put in quietly, remembering just how badly he hadn't wanted it—enough for it to end their marriage!

'Or wanted,' he accepted harshly. 'But there is a distinct difference between talking about a mythical baby and being presented with a *fait accompli!*'

A *fait accompli...*

Was that how Dominick thought of the child she carried?

Her mouth tightened angrily. 'Well, just put your mind completely at rest, Dominick, because this baby isn't yours!' In her mind it wasn't, because knowing as she did how Dominick felt about the prospect of fatherhood, this baby was *hers*. Hers, and no one else's.

Dominick felt as if all the air had been knocked out of his lungs and closed his eyes to block Kenzie out of his sight for the time it took him to regain his breath and fight down the nausea that rose up in his throat.

It wasn't his baby!

He wanted to shout, to rage, to hit out at someone, anyone, as the disappointment and pain threatened to overwhelm him.

How he had *wanted* Kenzie's baby to be his, how he had wanted Kenzie to come back to him.

And after the last five agonizing weeks of knowing he hated his life without her in it, he wouldn't have cared if it had only been the existence of the baby that made her come back.

But now he had lost her for ever. There was no way

she would ever want to come back to him when she was expecting another man's baby.

He straightened, forcing himself back under control as he looked at her. 'How do you think Carlton will feel about the baby?' he asked through gritted teeth.

Kenzie gave a dismissive laugh. 'I don't really think that's any of your business, Dominick.'

Maybe it wasn't, but he wanted to know anyway!

Carlton was shallow and selfish, and at forty-two had so far managed to avoid making a long-term commitment to any woman. And if Carlton didn't want Kenzie—

What was he thinking now?

That if Carlton didn't want her or the baby, maybe he could persuade Kenzie into coming back to him?

Kenzie decided she had had enough for one night, and needed to get away from Dominick, as far away as possible, in order to consider what she was going to do next.

'I think—' She broke off as a loud knocking sounded on the outer door.

'Masters, open the damn door!' Jerome shouted to accompany the knock. 'I know Kenzie is still in there and I want to talk to her!' he added as he rapped on the door again.

'No, don't bother to answer,' Kenzie told Dominick as he turned grimly to reach for the handle. 'I'm going back downstairs, anyway,' she announced lightly.

'Kenzie…?' Dominick questioned in surprise.

She stopped to give him a derisive smile. 'I told you not to worry about it, Dominick,' she said softly. 'I'm a big girl now, and more than capable of looking after myself and my baby, if the need arises.'

His mouth tightened. 'I'll kill him if he doesn't accept his responsibility—'

'And what would that achieve?' she asked.

'It would make me feel a whole lot better!' he snapped.

'I have no idea why.' Kenzie still smiled. 'Haven't you forgotten that you left Caroline on her own downstairs?' she reminded him ruefully.

'Caroline definitely *is* a big girl who can take care of herself!' he dismissed without concern.

'Kenzie, are you in there?' Jerome was rattling the door handle now.

'I really do have to go,' Kenzie told Dominick firmly. 'I—thank you for all your help earlier this evening,' she added briskly.

'You still haven't had anything to eat,' Dominick pressed impatiently.

'I'll order something downstairs,' she assured him. 'I—goodbye, Dominick.' She gave him one last shaky smile before leaving.

Just as if he were a stranger she had to offer polite thanks to, Dominick fumed once left on his own.

Was that what he was going to become to her in future? Would she marry Carlton once their own divorce was final, and so be lost to him for ever?

Could he really just stand by and let that happen?

Did he have a choice?

Yes, of course he had a choice. Kenzie had loved him once, maybe it wasn't too late for her to feel that way again.

Unlike five and a half months ago, he wasn't going to give her up without a fight…!

CHAPTER FIFTEEN

'WHAT are you doing here, Dominick?' Kenzie stared at him in amazement the next morning when she answered the doorbell of the apartment she rented while working in New York, and found him standing outside in the hallway. 'More to the point,' she added with a frown, 'how did you know where I was staying?'

Dominick looked less than his sartorially elegant self this morning, she thought, taking in his appearance. His dark hair was brushed back carelessly, his face was unshaven, and the shirt and jeans he wore looked as if he might have slept in them. If he had slept at all; the dark shadows beneath his eyes cast doubts upon that assumption.

He shrugged his broad shoulders. 'I asked Caroline—'

'And she just told you my New York address, did she?' Kenzie snapped sarcastically.

He smiled slightly. 'Along with a few words of abuse, yes!'

That wasn't too difficult to imagine considering the ridiculous accusation Caroline had made to Kenzie in the powder room the evening before about Dominick still being enthralled with her!

'What do you want, Dominick?' she queried guardedly, aware that Jerome was due to arrive any minute—probably to finish the argument they had begun once all the other guests had gone the evening before.

Dominick hadn't come back downstairs to the party the previous evening, and Kenzie could only conclude that was because he had had no wish to see her again after learning of her pregnancy.

Considering her own state of bemusement, Kenzie had just felt thankful that she didn't have to face him again, making sure she ate some food before renewing her role as the Carlton Cosmetics face, cheerfully brushing off the other guests' curiosity about her earlier collapse with the explanation that she 'must be getting a cold'. It was a lame excuse, but it was the best she had been able to come up with at the time!

Although Jerome had had plenty to say about it once all the guests had left...

Her mouth tightened as she remembered the argument that had ensued.

'Dominick?' she prompted sharply.

He shrugged, not really sure what he was doing here, except that he had wanted to see how Kenzie was this morning. After she had spoken to Carlton last night... 'I had a breakfast meeting, so I thought I would call to see how you are...?'

'I'm fine,' Kenzie answered warily, still eyeing his appearance with knit brows.

Dominick's mouth twisted wryly as he easily guessed the reason for that, but he hadn't been too concerned with impressing the person he had met for breakfast, hence his casual appearance.

He grimaced. 'I was also curious to know how Carlton took your news— Kenzie? You haven't told him yet, have you?' he realized slowly as she suddenly avoided meeting his gaze.

She sighed. 'Not yet, no,' she confirmed quietly. 'It wasn't exactly the right time last night,' she defended.

Dominick continued to stare at her. 'And what would you consider the right time to inform a man he's going to be a father?' He winced inwardly, thinking how just saying the words out loud felt as if he were beating himself with a stick!

Maybe if he kept saying it he would finally come to believe it was true!

He had spent a sleepless night pacing up and down his hotel suite trying to decide what to do next. One thing he was certain of was that he had to do something, and he knew that he couldn't just walk away from Kenzie without telling her how he felt. He owed her that much, at least.

She looked beautiful this morning, with her face bare of make-up, and her long hair pulled back in a pony-tail, wearing a bright pink tee shirt and faded figure-hugging jeans.

'Can I come in?' he prompted at her lack of reply. 'I could use a cup of coffee.'

Kenzie didn't want to invite him in; she didn't see the point of doing that. They had nothing left to say to each other.

Besides, Jerome was due to arrive at any moment, and the last thing she needed was for the two men to meet at her apartment. She was as unsure of Dominick's mood this morning as she had been last night, but one thing she was certain of was if the two men met Dominick was sure to challenge the other man over Kenzie's pregnancy.

And Jerome *knew* he couldn't be the father of her baby!

'There isn't any point in your coming in, Dominick,' she told him firmly, making no effort to relax her grip on the door as she kept him standing outside her apartment. 'I'm—going out later, anyway,' she added dismissively, not lying about that. She was flying back to England later on today...

'To talk to Carlton?' he probed.

She sighed her impatience. 'Again, that isn't any of your business, Dominick—'

'I'm making it my business,' he told her determinedly, easily pushing his way past her, into the apartment. 'You may not like it, Kenzie, but the fact is, you're still my wife, and—'

'If that's all that's bothering you, then sign the damn divorce papers and let's finish this once and for all!' she came back angrily, aware of the minutes ticking away.

If Dominick did challenge the other man over her pregnancy, then there was no way it wouldn't come out that Jerome couldn't possibly be the father of her baby!

Leaving only Dominick as a possible candidate...the man who had made it only too plain last night that he considered any child, his or anyone else's, as a 'responsibility'.

'And so leaving you free to marry Carlton!' Dominick snarled.

'This conversation is becoming extremely tiresome, Dominick.' She sighed impatiently.

'Don't you think he'll ask you?' Dominick felt goaded into challenging.

'Perhaps it doesn't really matter whether he asks me or not!'

Kenzie snapped back.

'And what the hell does that mean?' Dominick frowned darkly.

She shrugged. 'I'm rich, I'm independent, and having a baby on my own at this stage in my life really isn't going to be that much of a problem for me!'

No, Dominick had already worked that much out for himself during those hours of pacing his hotel suite the night before.

No doubt her family, her extremely loving close-knit family, would form ranks about her too.

'Look, Kenzie—' he ran an agitated hand through the dark thickness of his already tousled hair '—I didn't come here to argue with you—'

'No? Then what did you come here for?' she snapped. 'Because hard as I try, Dominick, I really can't see what any of this has to do with you!' She glared at him, twin wings of colour in her cheeks.

God, she was so beautiful it almost brought him to his knees, Dominick realized, feeling a deep ache within his body.

She looked even more slender today, emphasizing the fragility he had sensed in her last night, and without any make-up and her hair pulled back she appeared to be incredibly vulnerable.

He couldn't bear the thought of her trying to bring a child up on her own. Even if that child wasn't his.

'I came—' He broke off, swallowing hard. 'I came

because I just can't stay away from you!' he finally managed to get out, knowing by the confusion on Kenzie's face that she was as puzzled by the admission as he had been at about three o'clock this morning when he had acknowledged the painful fact to himself.

He really had been a fool five and a half months ago when he had let Kenzie walk away from him. And he didn't care if she was pregnant with Carlton's baby—he would be a fool all over again if he just let her go out of his life a second time!

Kenzie shook her head. 'I don't understand you, Dominick…'

'No,' he accepted ruefully, 'I don't suppose you do. I've been having a little trouble understanding myself lately. But—' he drew in a ragged breath before continuing '—Kenzie, if things don't work out between you and Carlton I want you to know—' The strident ringing of the doorbell interrupted him.

'That will be Jerome,' Kenzie told him hurriedly, feeling more confused than ever this morning by Dominick's lack of anger and derision. 'Dominick—'

'I'm not leaving, Kenzie,' he told her firmly. 'If you would prefer to talk to Carlton in private, then I'll go through to the kitchen or something, but I—I haven't finished talking to you myself yet. I'm not leaving,' he repeated decisively, the stubborn look on his face telling her that he meant what he said.

Dominick was different today, she realized, frowning as she had a sudden insight into what that difference was.

That 'ice man' that had been such a part of their argument five and a half months ago wasn't there…

The cold implacability of five weeks ago wasn't there…

Quite what that meant she wasn't sure, but surely it did mean something?

And what did he want her to know if things didn't work out between Jerome and herself…?

'Jerome isn't going to like your being here.' She sighed, knowing that didn't bother her unduly; Jerome had been less than his charming self last night as he had berated her for disappearing with Dominick in the way that she had—as if she had had any choice in the matter!—and she could only expect more of the same from him this morning.

'I don't give a—' Dominick broke off, drawing in a deeply controlling breath before continuing, 'Jerome Carlton's likes or dislikes are of absolutely no interest to me,' he dismissed derisively.

'*You're* the one that's important, Kenzie,' he added intently. 'You, and what you really want.'

He had reasoned last night that the Kenzie he knew couldn't have made love with him at Bedforth Manor in the way that she had if she was in love with another man. But did that mean that she had been in love with him then?

Kenzie continued to look at him for several searching seconds, giving an impatient groan as the doorbell shrilled out for a second time. 'Okay, Dominick, stay,' she accepted as she moved towards the door. 'But—oh, never mind!' she dismissed as she gave up on the idea of requesting that there not be any more arguments.

Dominick and Jerome argued every time they met, so why should today be any different?

'Kenzie!'

'Yes?' She turned back wearily, her eyes widening as Dominick strode forcefully across the room, his hands gentle as they moved up to cradle each side of her face as he looked down at her intently.

'Do you *want* to marry Carlton?' he asked huskily.

Kenzie closed her eyes to avoid the intensity of his gaze, knowing that she had misled him last night when she had told Dominick the baby she carried wasn't his.

'Kenzie, please!' he encouraged gruffly. 'Baby or not, do you want to marry Carlton?'

'Baby or not'…?

What did Dominick mean?

'Kenzie, for God's sake open your eyes and look at me!' he encouraged emotionally.

She raised her lids at last, looking deep into his eyes, searching, seeing—seeing—

What did she see…?

Something she didn't recognize. Something she had thought she would never see in Dominick's eyes. Something that made her breath catch in her throat.

'No,' she breathed shakily. 'No, I don't want to marry Jerome,' she admitted softly.

Dominick continued to examine her for several long seconds, just touching her like this making his hands tremble. 'Good,' he finally murmured. 'Because there is another alternative to marrying Carlton or bringing the baby up on your own.'

'There is…?' She frowned in confusion, still staring at him.

Dominick gave a rueful smile. 'It may not be one you want to take, but—I want you to know it's there nonetheless.' He drew in a ragged breath before continuing. 'You could stay married to me.'

Her eyes widened. 'But—'

'I should go and let Carlton in before he breaks the door down,' he encouraged, releasing her from his grip as Jerome thundered on the door again.

Kenzie was stunned, moving to answer the door as if in a daze, not absolutely sure what Dominick was saying to her, or why he was saying it.

Just as she wasn't certain what emotion she had seen in Dominick's eyes a few minutes ago, only knowing what her first instinct had been.

Love.

Bright.

Shining.

Intense.

Love…?

CHAPTER SIXTEEN

SHE must have been mistaken, Kenzie had convinced herself by the time she got to the door. Dominick didn't love anyone; he wouldn't allow himself to love anyone. Least of all her.

But if he didn't love her then why had he told her, when he believed she was expecting another man's baby, that she had the option of staying married to him…?

'About time,' Jerome snapped as she finally opened the door. He looked his usual suave self this morning in a dark suit and pale blue shirt with a neatly knotted blue and navy striped tie. 'What the hell do you mean by—'

'Would you come through to the sitting room, Jerome?' Kenzie made the request an order. 'I'm not accustomed to having conversations out in the hallway for everyone to hear.'

He scowled his displeasure. 'Maybe if you hadn't kept me waiting outside for ten minutes—'

'It was hardly ten minutes—'

'You—'

'I should accept Kenzie's invitation if I were you, Carlton,' Dominick growled from the doorway into the sitting room. 'My own would be far less polite!'

Jerome turned sharply to look at the other man, his gaze narrowing. 'I should have known! Spent the night, did you, Masters?' he taunted before giving Kenzie a derisive smile.

Kenzie felt her cheeks pale, having seen Jerome in a very different light last night.

'Whether or not I spent the night with my own wife is none of your damned business!' Dominick told Jerome harshly as he moved protectively to Kenzie's side, touching her arm lightly as he did so. 'Why don't we all go through to the other room and try to be civilized about this?' he prompted softly as he felt Kenzie tremble.

This sort of scene couldn't be good for her in her condition, he realized crossly. His presence here was probably making the situation worse, he acknowledged regretfully, at the same time knowing that he couldn't be anywhere else, that wherever Kenzie was in future was where he wanted to be too...

'Civilized?' Jerome Carlton repeated scornfully as he strode forcefully into the adjoining room. 'You made sure there was no possibility of that when you bought control of my company!'

'Of the *family*-controlled company,' Dominick corrected pointedly, at the same time maintaining his hold on Kenzie's arm.

'Yes, my family,' the other man said. 'And now you're the one calling the shots!'

Kenzie looked at the two men in frustration before moving away from Dominick to sit down in one of the armchairs.

All she had wanted to do this morning was smooth things over with Jerome before leaving New York to go back to England, away from both men. Instead the two of them were having an argument in her apartment, like stags clashing antlers!

An inevitable argument, she accepted. But she wished they could have chosen somewhere else to have it!

Dominick thrust his hands into his jeans pockets. 'And what if I'm not?' he challenged softly.

'Not what?' Jerome came retorted.

'The one calling the shots,' Dominick said mildly.

Kenzie looked at him in confusion, not understanding him any more than Jerome obviously did as he gave a disbelieving snort.

'Are you telling me that although you're now the major shareholder of Carlton Cosmetics you have no intention of interfering with my running of the company?' he said sceptically.

Dominick looked at the other man with mocking eyes. 'No, I'm not saying that at all—'

'I didn't think so!' Jerome Carlton snapped.

'Carlton, if you were any good at running the company then it would never have got into the difficulties it did a couple of years ago—'

'We got through that,' the other man defended.

'Only because you sold off forty-nine per cent of the shares and then contracted Kenzie to be your new face,' Dominick said provocatively. 'Your father built up the company, but since he retired five years ago and left it to your management it's been going steadily downhill—'

'That's a lie!' the older man came back angrily.

'It's the truth,' Dominick insisted quietly. 'You may be the eldest son and heir, but of Jack Carlton's two sons you aren't the one who should have been running Carlton Cosmetics the last five years.'

Jerome snorted. 'You think my little brother Adrian could have done better?'

'From the enquiries I've made, I know he could,' Dominick assured him grimly. 'I take it you haven't spoken to your brother this morning?' he added mildly.

'To Adrian?' the other man questioned in surprise. 'Why would I have?'

Yes, why would he? Kenzie wondered, mesmerized by this conversation in spite of herself.

Until the last few weeks she had only ever known Jerome as the charming sophisticate he chose to show, but having witnessed his behaviour last night and this morning she knew he was anything but that. Now he seemed to be nothing but a blustering bully who was completely outclassed by the calmly controlled Dominick.

The two men were so different in looks too, Jerome with all his golden boyish good looks, and Dominick so dark and brooding, but of the two Kenzie knew which one she had always preferred. There was simply no contest!

Although Dominick had always refused to believe that. Did he still believe that…?

Their conversation before she had answered the door to Jerome seemed to imply otherwise.

'I had breakfast with Adrian this morning,' Dominick informed them both. 'We had a very interesting meeting, and I believe when you next speak to him you will find that he is in possession of an extra fifty-one per cent of Carlton Cosmetics shares and as the major shareholder is now completely empowered to run the company as he sees fit.'

Kenzie gasped. Dominick's breakfast meeting this morning had been with Adrian Carlton, Jerome's younger brother…?

Jerome's handsome face darkened angrily. 'I don't believe you,' he finally replied. 'Adrian doesn't have the sort of money to buy that amount of shares.'

Kenzie could see, from Dominick's self-assured smile, that he was in fact telling the truth.

'Oh, he didn't buy them from me,' Dominick said sardonically. 'I'm signing them over to him later this afternoon. In exchange for his agreeing to release Kenzie from what's left of her contract.'

'You—'

'That was extremely arrogant of you, Dominick!' Kenzie gasped disbelievingly.

'You didn't let me finish, Kenzie,' he told her softly. 'Adrian will agree to release you from the contract only if you *choose* to be released,' he added firmly.

'And why would I want to do that?' She frowned.

'Because you're pregnant,' Dominick pointed out softly. 'How do you think you're going to carry on working when you're seven, eight months pregnant?'

'Surely that was for me to decide, not you?' She shook her head.

'You're pregnant?' Jerome interrupted coldly. '*That's* the reason you fainted last night?' He stared at her exasperatedly.

'That's the reason she fainted last night,' Dominick clarified, knowing that he hadn't explained himself to Kenzie properly, and that she saw his behaviour as high-handed. But really he was only trying to give her a let-out if she wanted one, the let-out he knew she had been seeking the last five weeks…

'I don't believe this!' Jerome shook his head as he began pacing the room impatiently. 'This is just—unbelievable,' he muttered inadequately. 'Did you get her pregnant on purpose?' he accused Dominick. 'Were you so determined to get her back that you made her pregnant to do it?' he scorned.

Kenzie's cheeks were flushed now. 'Don't be ridiculous, Jerome—'

'You did, didn't you?' Jerome took no notice of her as he scowled at Dominick.

'Jerome, don't be so—'

'No, let him speak, Kenzie,' Dominick cut in evenly, keeping very still as he looked at the other man through narrowed lids. 'What makes you so sure the baby is mine?'

Jerome snorted. 'Who else's would it be?' he snorted. 'Kenzie is so damned prudish she should take the veil! At least, she *could* have done,' he added insultingly. 'I'm not sure they accept pregnant nuns— What the hell—?' he choked as Dominick grasped him by his shirt front and all but lifted him off his feet. 'Take your hands off me, Masters!' he blustered as Dominick thrust his face into his.

Letting this man go was the last thing Dominick wanted to do as the truth hit him squarely in the chest. A truth Kenzie had always insisted upon, and which he had refused to believe!

He had taken this man's word over Kenzie's, and had instantly believed Carlton when he had told him that he and Kenzie were involved.

It had all been a lie!

A lie Carlton seemed to have forgotten completely in his anger.

'You lied to me, Carlton!' he denounced as he pushed the other man away from him. Touching Jerome Carlton now made him feel ill. 'Why did you tell me that you and Kenzie were having an affair?'

'You told him what?' Kenzie choked incredulously as she stared at Jerome in disbelief.

'I told him that the two of us were involved in a mad, passionate affair that was beyond both our controls,' Jerome sneered. 'And that the only reason you were hesitating about coming to New York with me was because you didn't want to hurt him!'

'But—but why would you do such a thing?' Kenzie questioned in a daze, completly shaken by this revelation.

At least it explained why Dominick had refused to believe her denials of the affair—how could he help but doubt her when Jerome was telling him completely the opposite? How must it have made Dominick feel to be told she was only staying with him out of a sense of pity?

To a man like Dominick, who didn't believe in love, that would have been the final humiliation...

Jerome shrugged, seeming unconcerned by his actions. 'Because selling off shares in Carlton Cosmetics wasn't enough to get the company out of trouble,' he told her unrepentantly. 'I needed something else, something bigger. What I came up with was the beautiful international model Kenzie Miller as the new face of Carlton Cosmetics. But I had to get your overbearing brute of a husband out of the picture first!'

Kenzie didn't think or hesitate as her hand arced upwards and made hard contact with Jerome's cheek, her eyes blazing with tears of anger as she glared her dislike at him.

His face twisted with derision as he put a hand up to his rapidly reddening face. 'Both of you seem to have lost the plot somewhere,' he muttered. 'The question both of you should really be asking yourselves isn't why I lied about my affair with Kenzie. The question you should be asking yourselves is why Masters found it so easy to believe me…'

The fact that he was right only made Dominick more angry.

'Get out, Carlton,' he grated harshly, his face pale, and eyes dark and haunted. 'Get out now. Before I give in to what I would really like to do to you!' he added bleakly before turning away, having eyes for no one but Kenzie.

Now he knew exactly what he had done and he knew also that Kenzie could never forgive him for the way he had doubted her.

Why should she? He had listened to, and believed, the word of a man who meant nothing to him, over the word of the woman who meant everything to him…

CHAPTER SEVENTEEN

'DOMINICK...?' Kenzie spoke uncertainly once the two
of them were alone, the apartment door having slammed
shut behind Jerome several seconds ago as he had
wisely taken Dominick's advice and left.

The verbal exchange between the two men had been
vicious, but for Kenzie so very enlightening...

She moistened her dry lips. 'Dominick, exactly when
did Jerome tell you he and I were having an affair?'

'Don't!' he groaned huskily, turning away to inhale
a deeply controlling breath. 'I—you—I was so wrong,
Kenzie!' he muttered in despair. 'So very wrong and so
arrogant. And I'm still doing it, aren't I?' he added self-
disgustedly. 'If you want to carry on working for Carlton
Cosmetics I'll tell Adrian this afternoon—'

'I don't,' she cut in impatiently, knowing that after
the things that had been said this morning, she could
never continue working for Carlton Cosmetics, even if
Adrian was now in charge of the company. 'What I
want is for you to answer my question.'

'You're angry.' Dominick sighed. 'You have every
right to be,' he accepted heavily, running a hand through

the dark thickness of his hair. 'What an idiot I've been,' he murmured. 'A stupid, stupid idiot! Can you ever forgive me, Kenzie?' He looked at her with pained eyes.

'I'm not sure there's really anything to forgive,' she said quietly.

'It sounds to me as if we were both manipulated by a totally unprincipled man who saw the rift in our marriage and took advantage of it.'

Dominick gave the ghost of a smile. 'That's very generous of you, Kenzie. I'm not sure, in the circumstances, that I could be as generous—'

'Dominick, please tell me when Jerome told you those awful lies about the two of us,' she prompted tensely.

'It was after one of our—uglier arguments.' He grimaced at the memory. 'It's difficult to remember which one. We were arguing such a lot in that month before we separated. Ironically over having the baby you are now expecting,' he acknowledged ruefully.

Yes, ironically, Kenzie also realized.

A baby that she already loved, but had no idea how Dominick, now that he must realize the baby was his too, felt about it...

Dominick shook his head in disgust. 'I was always so determined never to fall in love, never to lay myself open to the sort of pain my parents had inflicted on each other and on me!' He sighed deeply. 'Even when I asked you to marry me I reasoned it all out so logically! I was thirty-seven. A wife, especially one as beautiful and accomplished as you, could be a good business asset. I wanted you, you wanted me, so why not get married? God, what an arrogant fool I was! Okay,' he drawled self-derisively as he saw Kenzie smile slightly, 'what an arrogant fool I still am!'

'Do you think?' Kenzie prompted softly.

'No, I don't,' he said heavily. 'Those first four months without you were indescribable! I told myself it was because I was angry. Furious. And with good reason. Not only had you walked out on me, but you had left me to go to New York with another man.'

'Because Jerome lied to you about the two of us having an affair...' Kenzie frowned, half of her knowing that what Jerome had said—taunted—was true: if she and Dominick had had the sort of marriage where they loved and trusted each other, then none of that misunderstanding would have happened...

'We barely spoke any more,' Dominic went on, 'let alone made love. We were like two polite strangers sharing the same apartment. And then when you seemed so determined you were going to accept the contract Carlton Cosmetics were offering you I decided to go and speak to Carlton myself. What the hell I thought I was doing, I have no idea.' He grimaced at the thought. 'The man I was then seems like someone else to me.' He winced. 'A cold, arrogant man who seemed to think the whole world, but especially you, should comply with what I wanted. Even when it came to having children...' he added heavily.

'We can talk about the baby in a minute,' Kenzie assured him, a tiny bubble of happiness starting to grow inside her, getting bigger with every passing second. 'What's important is that you believe Jerome lied,' she said firmly. 'That you believe I have never had an affair. With him or anyone else.'

'How can I not believe you?' he groaned. 'But, don't you see? I should have known it *then!* If I had trusted you then, if I had believed in the love you said you felt for me, then—'

'You hadn't had too much of an example of love up to that point in your life, Dominick—'

'Don't make excuses for me, Kenzie,' he muttered, interrupting her. 'I behaved abominably when you said you were going ahead and accepting the contract despite what I said. I behaved even more dreadfully six weeks ago by taking advantage of the situation when you came and asked for my help over Kathy's wedding,' he acknowledged hollowly.

Yes, he had. But if, despite Kenzie's denials, Jerome had told him that the two of them were having an affair, she could see how hard it would have been for Dominick, when their own relationship was so strained by that time, to have believed anything else.

If the two of them had loved each other, if they had been secure in that love, then no one, and nothing, would have been able to come between them to destroy that love…

'I don't blame you for hating me now, Kenzie,' Dominick said flatly at her continued silence. 'It's the least I deserve after the way I've behaved.' He closed his eyes briefly, dull pain in their depths when he opened them again to look at her. 'If I could take it all back, if I could undo what I've done— Damn it, no matter what I thought the provocation, I had no right to treat you the way that I did. Not six months ago. And certainly not five weeks ago when I forced you to come away with me to Bedforth Manor.' His face was very pale. 'I bought that house for you, Kenzie. Just before you left me.'

Dominick had bought that wonderful, warm, *family* home for her…?

'It doesn't make a lot of sense, does it?' he acknowledged as he saw her obvious surprise. 'I'd had this vision of taking you there, of telling you I had bought it for the two of us to live in, of seeing your face light up in the way that it used to when you were happy…' He shook his head. 'And instead, four months later I forced you to go there with me and—'

'Dominick,' Kenzie cut in softly. 'You have to stop this now. It isn't helping anything, least of all us, to rip yourself apart like this.'

'I told you, it's what I deserve!' he bit out forcefully.

'Why don't you let me be the one to decide what you deserve?' she whispered huskily.

He gave a humourless smile. 'Okay, Kenzie, tell me what you think I deserve?' His shoulders tensed as if for a blow.

'I will,' she promised gently. 'Dominick, when we first met I fell completely, irrevocably, unreservedly, in love with you.'

'I know that!' He gave a pained groan. 'It was a love I believed I was totally incapable of returning!'

Had believed he was incapable of returning…?

That past tense gave her the encouragement she needed. 'What you don't seem to be aware of is that I'm still completely, irrevocably, unreservedly in love with you!' She smiled shakily.

Dominick became very still, his heart beating so loudly it threatened to deafen him.

'I could never have made love with you at Bedforth Manor in the way that I did if I wasn't still in love with you,' Kenzie continued softly. 'The baby I'm carrying—our baby—was, as far as I'm concerned, conceived in love.'

He swallowed hard, his emotions—admiration for Kenzie, a building joy, but mostly love—overwhelming him.

'Dominick, before Jerome arrived, you said I had another alternative,' she reminded huskily. 'You offered to continue our marriage even believing that I was expecting another man's baby. Dominick, did you offer that because you—you love me? Please answer me, Dominick!' she pleaded emotionally.

'Yes, I love you!' He took a hesitant step towards her. 'I know now that I've always loved you. Since the moment I first looked at you. Since the moment you first smiled at me. I just didn't realize it until I made love with you at Bedforth Manor. Our lovemaking that day was so overwhelming, so deeply moving, it was completely unlike anything else we had ever shared!'

'For me too,' she admitted quietly.

He swallowed hard. 'Please believe me when I say I've changed, Kenzie! That I really do love you. That I'll love you until the day I die,' he said with certainty, the last five and a half months without her showing him exactly how much he loved and needed her.

She reached up to caress one hard cheek. 'I do believe you, Dominick,' she choked. 'I really do.'

He breathed raggedly. 'I want you to know our baby—a baby I assure you I want very, very much!—was conceived in love on my part too!' he whispered. 'We made love that day, my darling—and it scared the hell out of me!'

Kenzie didn't seem to notice the tears falling down her cheeks as she laughed huskily. 'Then what you deserve, Dominick, what we both deserve, is a second chance at being together. And this time we'll get it right!' she promised determinedly.

'Do you really mean that, Kenzie?' He stared at her. 'You'll take me back? Give me a second chance? Let me be a father to our child?'

'All of those things, Dominick,' she said, gulping back her tears. 'And this time we won't let anything, or anyone, come between us!'

Dominick no longer cared whether or not he deserved this second chance, he just intended grabbing it with both hands and never letting go!

'I love you!' he groaned as he took her in his arms and held her tightly against him. 'I love you. I love you. I love you!' He rained kisses all over her face, first her eyes, then her nose, and finally her mouth, kissing her with all the love he had inside him for this beautiful, forgiving woman.

He still had a lot to learn about love, but he didn't doubt that Kenzie would show him how, together, in honesty and trust, the two of them could do anything…

'Can we live at Bedforth Manor?' Kenzie asked him a long time later. 'I absolutely love the house. And the pool-house. It's where our baby was conceived, after all,' she added teasingly, the two of them now snuggled up together on the sofa, Dominick's arms about her as he held her tightly against him.

'I don't care where I live as long as I'm with you,' Dominick stated fiercely, knowing a happiness that he had never believed possible, the past gone now as he realized at long last that to be truly happy he had to give love as well as receive it.

And he loved Kenzie more than life itself.

Their baby was the result of that love. And their child would grow up knowing its parents loved it as much as they loved each other.

'Why don't we arrange to renew our wedding vows? In the same church where your sisters were all married?' he encouraged softly, loving the silky feel of her hair as he caressed the smooth darkness.

Kenzie turned to look up at him. 'Would you really like that…?'

'Yes, I would,' he assured her without hesitation. 'I would like to do this properly this time, Kenzie. Most of all I would like to share promising to love you for the rest of our lives with all of your family.'

'Then that's what we'll do,' she agreed, overwhelmed with the happiness they had now found together.

Dominick smiled down at her. 'I've also been thinking that I might like to buy an estate agency in Worcestershire… In the name of a company, so that your father doesn't realize it's me, of course. What do you think?'

She kissed him lightly on the lips. 'I think you had better not reform too much, Dominick, or I won't recognize you any more!' she teased lovingly.

'Hmm,' he murmured, his own face softened with the same emotion. 'Perhaps we should go into the bedroom and refresh our memories…?'

'Perhaps we should.' Kenzie stood up, holding out her hand to him. 'There's more than one way of renewing our vows to each other,' she whispered huskily as the two of them walked hand in hand to the bedroom.

Their daughter, Sophie Louise, was born eight months later, tears of happiness falling down Dominick's cheeks as the tiny miracle was placed into his arms.

She was so beautiful, this daughter of his.

So perfect.

So exactly like her mother in every way he decided as he looked lovingly at Kenzie.

The love of his life…

THE ROYAL HOUSE OF NIROLI

...International affairs, seduction and passion guaranteed

Volume 1 – July 2007
The Future King's Pregnant Mistress by Penny Jordan

Volume 2 – August 2007
Surgeon Prince, Ordinary Wife by Melanie Milburne

Volume 3 – September 2007
Bought by the Billionaire Prince by Carol Marinelli

Volume 4 – October 2007
The Tycoon's Princess Bride by Natasha Oakley

8 volumes in all to collect!